"*For a moment there, you made me forget everything.*"

Leo continued. "We were lovers again—but lovers as we'd never been before. And then I realized that some other man—or men—must have been teaching you the art of love."

"No!" she wailed.

"I wish I could believe you!" he said fervently. "*I* wanted to be that man, Ginny!"

"Leo, I—I wanted you to...care for me, to help me," she jerked out.

"Sure. You let me have you because you wanted something. Now I *do* believe the stories about you."

"I am innocent, Leo," she said, wondering if she could ever crack that icy regard.

"I should have seen it coming. I can't entirely blame you. That's the kind of world you entered. But you're right. Our worlds don't mix. Pack your things. You've got an hour to be out of here. Leave nothing behind to remind me of a very bad mistake I made. We're finished, Ginny."

Dear Reader,

Welcome to Sara Wood's colorful new trilogy. The series is full of family intrigue, secrets, lies and, of course, love. It involves the St. Honoré family, which has a reputation second to none in Saint Lucia. Mandy, Ginny and Amber are drawn into this notorious family and the secrets of its past. Each of these intrepid heroines is looking for love and each of them will find it—but only where they least expect it! But then, as you'll discover, in this series things are rarely as they seem!

In *White Lies* (#1910), Mandy Cook is desperate to find her father, and perhaps Vincente St. Honoré can help her. If she can ever find him! For first she must wrest herself from the arms of his commanding and charismatic son—Pascal.

In *Scarlet Lady*, Ginny MacKenzie is a successful fashion model, but her worst nightmares are confirmed as she is wrongly branded a scarlet lady by the press and loses her husband, the Hon. Leo Brandon, as a result. It is only when, two years later, she decides to search for love elsewhere that Ginny is reunited in Saint Lucia with the man she has always loved—Leo! The question is, why is he there?

In *Amber's Wedding* (#1922), Amber Fraser has just married Jake Cavendish, not for love but for convenience, companionship and to secure a father for her unborn child. On their wedding day Jake reveals to Amber a secret that will change her life. A secret that will finally reveal the truth about the St. Honoré family. They honeymoon in Saint Lucia where love appears to blossom after all—until Amber discovers *Jake's* real motive for marrying her. You can read Amber's story in November 1997.

Happy reading!

The Editor

SARA WOOD

Scarlet Lady

Harlequin Books

TORONTO • NEW YORK • LONDON
AMSTERDAM • PARIS • SYDNEY • HAMBURG
STOCKHOLM • ATHENS • TOKYO • MILAN
MADRID • WARSAW • BUDAPEST • AUCKLAND

ISBN 0-373-11916-X

SCARLET LADY

First North American Publication 1997.

With my grateful thanks to Mrs. Joan Devaux,
Gary Devaux, Maria Monplaisir
and all at Anse Chastanet

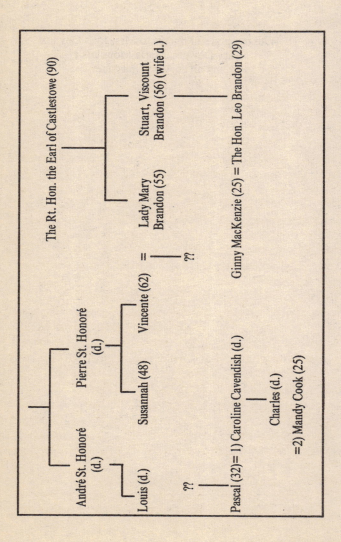

The Rt. Hon. the Earl of Castlestowe (90)

André St. Honoré (d.)

Pierre St. Honoré (d.)

Louis (d.)

Susannah (48)

Vincente (62)

= ??

Lady Mary Brandon (55)

Stuart, Viscount Brandon (56) (wife d.)

?? Pascal (32) = 1) Caroline Cavendish (d.)

Charles (d.)

=2) Mandy Cook (25)

Ginny MacKenzie (25) = The Hon. Leo Brandon (29)

CHAPTER ONE

SHE'D lost. To the tune of nearly a million pounds in costs. A million pounds! Ginny sat frozen and immobile while the words roared around her head and slowly, brutally their meaning became clear. All her efforts to make herself financially independent—the self-denial, the relentless sacrifices which had begun to threaten her marriage—were to be wiped away by a judge's decision.

Her perfectly painted mouth trembled. The sacrifices had been too great. She'd lost almost everything because she'd decided to sue the newspaper which had printed outrageous lies about her. The court had upheld the journalist's story and she had been ordered to pay all of the defendant's costs.

Yet she was innocent! Ginny all but sobbed in despair. She loved her husband—and her self-respect—too much to sleep around. It appalled her that anyone would believe she'd furthered her career by doing so.

As the room whirled in a kaleidoscope of colour, a friendly arm came around her shoulder. 'Ginny,' said her bodyguard gently, 'let's get out of here, huh?'

The arm steadied her. Now she focused on a sea of faces, all looking at her. She was used to scrutiny, though not for *this* reason. From force of habit she smoothed her face of any revealing expression and eased down her breathing till it was normal.

'Sure, Chas,' she said evenly. And she thought that few people must realise how hard she had to work to control her voice, her eyes, her limbs as she uncoiled her

near-six-foot length and gracefully shrugged on a fake
fur coat against the bitter cold that awaited outside. 'Take
me home,' she said gratefully, aware that only Chas knew
how badly she was shaking and how deeply the verdict
had wounded her sense of decency and pride.

She needed Leo. Her darling husband. The man she'd
loved from the moment their eyes had first met. It was
all she could think of—Leo's arms around her, comforting her, cradling her and murmuring soothing words
of tender love.

The Press were already exploding flashes in her face,
even in the courtroom, shouting cruel questions that
made her wince. Like 'Where's your husband, Ginny?'
That hurt. If only he'd been by her side instead of ad-
ministering an estate that had managers galore!

She drew in her breath when she thought of Leo and
how disappointed she'd felt when he hadn't been prepared to accept her preoccupation with this case. She'd
realised that he couldn't completely abandon
Castlestowe, but she'd *needed* him. Leo's continued absence during the trial had been like a dagger in her heart.

She'd been nineteen when they'd married and for four
wonderful years they had loved one another with a
passion that had had her floating on air. He'd been kind,
gentle and cherishing. Her empty soul had flowered with
his love. It was the first time in her life that she'd felt
truly whole.

He'd been eager in the old days to hurry back to their
London home after his visits to the family seat in
Scotland. And when she'd returned from an assignment
abroad he'd be waiting at the airport, arms full of
flowers, and exciting boxes at his feet containing perfume
and silk fripperies, his handsome face alight with love.

Her eyes glowed with memories. Deep down he was sensitive. He'd see how upset she was. He'd put Castlestowe to one side and take her in his arms and their differences would be forgotten. Their love would knit them together again.

Slowly she walked out of the courtroom with the famous seamless stride that made her slender body flow within her beautifully cut cerise suit—the stride and sway which had won her the title of Catwalk Model of the Year.

'Ginny! Over here... Ginny! Give us a flash of yer legs! Where's old Leo, darlin'? Ginny! Here, Ginny...!'

Knowing that she'd be pestered mercilessly otherwise, she gave the Press a minute or two more, maintaining her serene calm and the same elegant tilt of her blonde head that had prompted the media to dub her 'the new Grace Kelly'. It had taken her a while to force her own name on the public consciousness but at last she had become *the* Ginny McKenzie.

Few ever mentioned the fact that she was a Brandon by marriage, Leo being the son of Viscount Brandon. Her refusal to change her name had caused trouble with his family—but how could she have done that when it had taken her so much effort to become recognised? It would have been professional suicide.

'Here, Gin! Over here! Good girl! Look at me, babe!'

'They think you're a dog, or somethin'?' growled Chas.

'Their property,' she said ruefully. And steadied her voice. No outsider must know how she felt. 'OK. That's enough. If they can't get a decent photo out of those shots, they don't deserve a job. Get me out of here,' she begged.

And she clamped a hand on her Garboesque brimmed hat as Chas manoeuvred her through the pushing crowds to the waiting limo.

'Hell,' he muttered. 'I don't know how you stand this!'

Exhausted, she pulled down the blinds to shut out the excited faces outside. Fans and enemies. The envious and the angry. And she wondered how she stood it. And why. Was it worth it?

When the car had picked up a little speed and Sue, the chauffeuse, began to weave in and out of the back streets to throw followers off the scent, Ginny finally let out a long, heartfelt groan and slumped into the white leather cushions.

'I can't believe it,' she said. 'I'm innocent and I'm being forced to pay the court costs for a disgusting tabloid which printed lies about me!'

Chas took her hand, his blue eyes angry, and leaned close in sympathy. 'I wish I could help. I'm— Damn!' he swore as a blinding flash illuminated their faces. 'Stop the car!' he yelled, clambering over Ginny as Sue screeched to a halt.

Ginny felt her heart sink. Neither of them had noticed that the blind had shot up, that they'd been stationary and waiting for traffic lights to turn green. Or that a photographer had managed to tail them and take a shot of Chas's kind consolation. Miserably she waited for Chas to return, knowing that the photographer had already vanished and there would be another scoop in the papers.

She shivered, her enormous eyes glistening with unshed tears. Achieving success beyond most people's wildest dreams had brought with it a load of trouble.

'I'll chuck it all in,' she said shakily to no one in particular.

'And give them cause to think you're guilty?' called Sue indignantly over her shoulder.

'They already do!' Ginny drew in a sharp, despairing breath and waited while Chas slid back into the car. 'I want Leo!' she groaned.

'Won't be long. Come on,' soothed Chas.

An arm reached across her, pulling down the blind again. And then she was being eased into Chas's concrete-like chest, where she snuffled and tried to hold back her tears till she heard the sound of iron gates clanging back. St John's Wood, exclusive and protected. Home. And Leo—perhaps. She stilled her racing pulses ruthlessly because she dared not hope too much.

'Thanks,' she said huskily to Chas. He was a dear. Solid, East End decent. 'Sue, slowly, please. I need a moment to tidy up.'

Butterflies beat themselves against the walls of her stomach when she saw Leo's car slewed across the driveway ahead. A joy filled her heart. The trial was over. Good or bad, it meant that the pressure on her time was off. She and Leo could spend time together, heal their marriage. The thought of seeing him made her heart pump rapidly.

And she remembered the joyful days they'd spent together, loving and laughing, such good friends, so close, so happy. A frown dipped her arched brows. Once he'd been her rock. Now she felt uncertain as to her welcome.

With trembling, suddenly clumsy fingers, she flicked out the hanging mirror and nervously whisked ash-blonde strands back into the severe chignon, then re-touched the mascara on her endless lashes and reshaped her pink mouth. There was a vulnerability and a paleness about her face that hadn't been there before. Now her cheekbones seemed even sharper, the hollows beneath more pronounced.

Jamming her hat back on her head and shrugging her coat collar up high, she said huskily, 'OK, Sue. I'm decent.' And felt like a girl on her first date. Scared. Excited. Quivering.

Disappointment hit her when she saw that Leo wasn't waiting for her on the mansion steps when they swept up. George, the butler, was, however, with the cook and the maid and the gardener, all with loving concern on their faces. They were fond of her but their sympathy when she swung her long legs from the limo was almost too much to bear.

It crossed her mind that her staff currently cared for her more than her husband did. And they believed she was innocent.

Perhaps he was on the phone. Maybe he'd telephoned the solicitor so that he'd know the verdict before she arrived home—or he was fending off the media. Calmer, she felt glad that she'd chosen the sleek, tailored suit. It was Leo's favourite.

Warmth flowed through her. They'd cuddle and he'd tell her that he loved her and nothing else mattered. Then they'd go to bed and he'd hold her tightly and everything would be all right. She felt better already.

'Leo around?' she asked George eagerly when everyone had said how sorry, how shocked they were and offered their help wherever it might be needed.

'In the library, Ginny,' he answered with more than usual tenderness.

'Fine,' she lied, suddenly wary. Why was George looking at her like that? 'And...thanks, everyone, for your support. I do appreciate it. It makes a lot of difference to the way I feel. Bless you all.'

Still smiling, wanting to let her composure go and to give in to the newly arrived apprehension, she wriggled out of her coat, flung her hat on the marquetry table and glided to the library.

But, positioned at the far end of the long room, by the window, her beloved Leo was smiling down at a woman who sat on the window-seat: Arabella Lake, fellow model, rival, and a mean manhunter. And neither of them even noticed her arrival because they were both so engrossed in one another.

Shocked, Ginny clutched the jamb of the door, almost at the end of her tether. Arabella! Her eyes closed in dismay then opened reluctantly at his soft, husky laugh. She wanted comfort. Needed his arms around her. Instead, she'd have to listen to Arabella's false condolences and know that the malicious woman was delighting in Ginny's failure to clear her name.

'Leo!' she called, her voice low and husky with misery.

He looked up, his eyes brooding, nodded curtly in cold acknowledgement, then continued to smile and chat to Arabella. Ginny walked the long gallery as if she were on hot coals and naked before a jeering audience, her stomach somewhere in her boots, her pulses jittering so badly that she could hardly keep her balance.

It struck her forcibly that it had been a long time since Leo had looked at her with the same smiling affection that he was showing towards Arabella. When he'd glanced towards her just now, his face falling into icily disapproving lines, he'd seemed almost a stranger. Nervous and inwardly panicking, she gazed at his beloved face, seeing what Arabella was seeing.

A tall man, one of the few who could tower over tall models like herself—and Arabella. Thick hair the colour of rich brown silk, swept back from his face and cut to perfection. Tanned and healthy from an outdoor life on the estate. His brows strongly defined and often imperious, a long, straight nose of aristocratic hauteur and steadily piercing eyes that drowned women in their smoky, smouldering depths. And a projection of masculinity and natural, centuries-old authority and self-confidence that drew women to him like a magnet.

They'd called him Charisma, at Eton. It was obvious why and her heart lurched as her adoring eyes followed the sharp line of his jaw and lingered on the full mouth with an upper lip that could have been chiselled from marble like the statues in Castlestowe Castle.

She wanted to fling herself at him, to press her mouth to his. But something held her back—a fear of rejection so strong that she faltered, unable to continue for a moment.

And then she walked on, feeling the pull of Leo's earthy sexuality and wondering whether Arabella felt it too. Stupid! Of course she did! There had always been a rawness about him that transcended the conventional politeness of his impeccable breeding. It had forced her to face her own passion, to give out a little of the fire—but not all; she didn't dare—that her adoptive parents had all but driven out of her at an early age. And now she could see that he was deliberately projecting that overt sexuality—to Arabella.

The corners of her mouth drooped in misery when she heard him talking to Arabella in the tone of voice he used in bed—as if he'd spent too long in a smoke-filled room. She saw the intense look, the total concentration, as if his hungry grey eyes could look nowhere else...

He's *mine*! she thought furiously. 'Hello, Arabella.' Her shaky greeting won her a brief, cold smile from the smirking woman but no other acknowledgment. Leo seemed to have superglued his gaze to Arabella's, Ginny thought glumly.

She knew that he'd been annoyed over the trial even taking place. The lawsuit had begun two years ago and she'd been forced to juggle extended modelling dates and sessions with her lawyer till she'd hardly seemed to be at home at all—and when she had been she'd felt exhausted. Leo had complained. Eventually he'd asked her to work part-time and settle down on the estate in Scotland. Which he loved and she hated. It was bleak and wet and isolated.

'The verdict came in, Leo,' she said quietly, breathing evenly to eliminate the shake from her voice.

'I know. I got a call from a journalist asking my opinion of Chas,' he said curtly.

Ginny paled, knowing that the scene in the car would have been embellished out of all proportion. 'Can I talk to you in private for a moment or so?' she asked faintly.

'If you wish.'

Leo's indifferent tones cut her like a knife. The humiliation was so intense that she felt like turning tail and running from the room, but Arabella was already rising to her feet and wrapping her arms around Leo's neck.

'Poor Ginny,' sighed Arabella, her green eyes slanting maliciously. 'I hear she'll be bankrupt. I guess she's lost everything she lives for. I'll slip away for a while. Bye for now, darling,' she cooed, then planted her scarlet lips firmly on Leo's and kept them there for several seconds.

'Catch you later,' said Leo calmly, emerging from the clinch. His hands stayed on Arabella's waist, Ginny noticed jealously. And he was smiling beautifully, letting his eyes twinkle. Or were they kindling? she thought jealously. But, whatever they were doing, it wasn't for her. 'Tea will be served in the drawing room in an hour. See you then.'

He smiled when Arabella gave him a flirty flutter of her talons and tottered off in a skirt that was indecently short.

'Is...?' Ginny frowned. 'Is Arabella staying for tea?' she asked in dismay.

'Staying—' Leo turned an unreadable gaze on her '—for a few days.'

When she needed privacy to lick her wounds! 'You...invited her?'

The long dark fringe of lashes flickered. 'You have a problem with that?' he asked.

'I—I wanted us to be alone,' Ginny began miserably.

'I've been alone for too long. I wanted company.' Leo's eyes only warmed when they watched Arabella's slow progress—a kind of exaggerated cat-walk down the long gallery.

Ginny tried to smile without much success. He seemed to be telling her something. And she didn't want to hear it. The implication was that he needed a woman around who'd give him what she'd been incapable of giving for some time: love, companionship, quality time...sex.

Her tawny eyes flickered with pain. They hadn't made love—not *real* love, sweet and tender—since the tabloid article had come out. And she'd been too scared to ask if he didn't care any more. Her heart pounded violently. If that were true, she'd go to pieces. It would be the end of her world.

Once, twice, he'd made love to her as if he hardly knew her, in a restrained way that had left her crying alone in the great bed while he'd disappeared to take a shower. She'd imagined that he was washing her off his body. How long was it since they'd last slept together?

She couldn't even remember, knowing only that she missed his loving arms and felt terribly alone.

Appalled, Ginny waited in the cold, unfriendly silence till Arabella's merrily clicking heels had stopped driving her crazy and the door had closed at the far end of the room. Leo was wiping lipstick from his mouth. And the cool neutrality had gone and he was suddenly very, very angry.

He had no right to be! Surely he must know what an ordeal she'd been through, how hard it had been to hold herself together these past few months? She was his wife and she was in trouble!

'Leo... I know it's been hard for you—hard for both of us—but... right at this moment I need you,' she said brokenly.

His bitter, glittering eyes slanted in her direction. 'Is that how it works?' he growled, and faced her at last, his face working with anger, the mouth that had so recently softened under Arabella's now a hard, unpleasant line carved in Scottish granite. 'I've needed you, Ginny. I've needed your support, your time, an understanding ear. I was happy for you to have a career but I didn't expect it to take you over completely. And this trial and the rumours about you—'

'Leo!' she said quickly, terrified of where this was leading. 'They're not true...' Her voice tailed away at his tormented expression.

'Ginny,' he said quietly, 'you must know how deeply you've hurt me and my family.'

She turned away. Leo's family had always unnerved her. His grandfather, the Earl of Castlestowe, had made it clear that he'd expected her to drop her career and concentrate on producing heirs.

'I never wanted to hurt anyone you care about. I love you,' she said unhappily, trembling, trying to remember how it had felt to be loved back. There was nothing but emptiness now—a blank feeling as if he'd wiped her clean and left a vacuum. 'I married you because I couldn't live without you. I still feel like that.'

He thrust his hands in the pockets of his linen trousers and stood silhouetted against the huge, mullioned window, a picture of power, money and perfect lineage. Chills ran down her spine. He was regretting their marriage. She didn't fit, never had done. Wrong class. Wrong blood. Oh, God! she screamed inside.

'You seem to have managed fine without me for some time,' he said huskily. 'What do you think that tells me, Ginny?'

'Please try to understand,' she said, horrified at how far they'd drawn away from one another. 'I love you but I need to work for my self-respect—'

'We talked of children,' he reminded her. 'You knew how much I wanted us to have a child.'

Ginny winced. She was scared of motherhood and what it implied, because their child would never be hers to love. They wouldn't be having a baby. They'd be producing an heir. And almost certainly her duty would be to bring up the Brandon heir according to the strict Brandon rules and regulations.

She knew something of Leo's childhood: the nannies who'd ruled his life till he'd been sent to boarding-school, the cold baths and rigorous devotion to duty. Leo had touched her heart when he'd told her that his mother had never cuddled him and had died in a riding accident when he was five.

Her own childhood had been hell too. No way was she going to inflict misery on her own flesh and blood in the same way. When she had a child, she wanted to be free to give it the love that she and Leo had been denied. But first their marriage had to be strong.

'You know why we delayed—'

'Your figure. Your career,' he said accusingly.

She stiffened. 'No! that isn't true! Leo, I never knew you could be so cruel—'

'I was never cuckolded before!' he said tightly.

She gasped in dismay and scanned the cold, bleak face for some sign of pity. None. Only that merciless glare. Pain seared through her. 'No man has ever made love to me but you!' she replied vehemently, her fingers picking fretfully at the pearl buttons of her suit. The curl of his mouth grew more contemptuous. 'You have to believe me, Leo!' she cried passionately, near to hysterics.

'How can I ever know?' he shot back.

The question shafted through her like a knife. Ginny raised sorrowful, gold-shot eyes to his, begging for a shred of affection that she could cling to. 'I can't prove anything,' she said in a whisper. 'Not to you, the public, my friends, your family, the courts. I was hoping—' She broke off and took a moment to find control of her voice. 'I lost the case,' she croaked. 'I have to pay nearly a million in costs,' she continued, hoping for some hint that he might want to console her.

'I told you not to resort to litigation,' he said in exasperation.

'Don't men normally defend their wife's honour?' she asked, her near-hysteria making her sound a little sharp.

'Against the tabloids?' One peat-brown eyebrow expressed scorn and disagreement. 'That's not how it's done, Ginny. It would be tantamount to saying that their lies could have an effect. Ignoring them is more dignified. You went against my advice and now you're reaping the consequences.'

'And you mean to chastise me like a disobedient child?' she retorted. 'Can't you see I need—?'

'No. I won't throw Brandon money at you any more. You have your own account; use it,' he said flatly.

Tears trickled down her cheeks and into the corners of her parted lips. 'Oh, drat!' she rasped angrily, knuckling them away, not caring if her eye make-up became smudged. 'Leo, I wasn't asking for money; I'll earn more if I have to—do shows, TV interviews, anything—but...I...'

Overwhelmed, she reached out her arms to him in a piteous gesture. He ignored her plea. She knew that he was stubborn. Once, he'd defied his family to marry her and had defended her when they didn't rush to produce children as soon as everyone expected. And once he'd admired her success.

Now they no longer had the same goals, she thought miserably. Their lives were drawing apart. They had become strangers and he didn't want to defend her any more.

'Your career means a lot to you,' he observed.

'Naturally,' she said huskily. 'I've worked hard. It's given me self-esteem, Leo!'

'I know that. I don't denigrate what you've done. I've been proud of you.' His hooded eyes brooded on her. 'But...you can't be everything to all people and do it well, Ginny,' he said in a gentler tone than before.

'I had to try!' she cried in exasperation. 'Don't you see? If I hadn't kept my name up top and continued with the shows during the run-up to the trial, I'd have been yesterday's face in the twinkling of an eye. And what else would I do?' she asked hotly. 'You don't seriously think I could sit around all day discussing menus and arranging flowers, do you?'

'Don't be ridiculous!' he growled.

Ginny drove her teeth into her lower lip, knowing that she'd been unfair. He'd never asked that of her. 'What do you want from me?' she asked.

'Exclusivity,' he rasped rawly.

She controlled the urge to wince. 'I am yours. Wholly yours.'

'Are you?'

Her mouth trembled. It was clear that he didn't believe her. 'My darling, can't we start again? Please hold me. I need your arms around me so badly—'

'And I've needed yours many times and you've not been there,' he said quietly. 'It's not a marriage any more—'

'It will be!' she cried in panic, her hand pressing her chest where her heart banged painfully against her ribs. 'It's been a bad time but we can be together again—'

'We both have to want that,' he muttered.

Her eyes rounded in horror. His serious expression scared her. Cold to the bone, she dreaded to be told that he didn't love her any longer. She tried to speak but could only croak out a plaintive little 'Leo!'

'It's true, Ginny,' he muttered, the line of his mouth as wintry as the atmosphere at Castlestowe. 'I'm not sure you understand how to live and behave normally any more. Ever since you began to hit the big time, you've been spinning into orbit and getting more out of control as the years go by. And now you're famous people fix things for you. Hair, teeth, nails. They wax your legs, drive you wherever you want to go, arrange your accommodation, whisk you to parties and even dress you!'

'It's not like that!' she protested. 'You and the public only see what the film crews want you to see! People dashing around trying to look important and making sure they get into camera shot!'

'But it's an unreal life,' he insisted. 'What the hell do you know about something as everyday as marriage? You don't realise it takes nurturing and nourishing to keep it alive and on fire!' he cried, his voice rising. 'Every time there's a picture of you with some leering film star or politician I get sniggers from people I know, and I can tell they're wondering if I believe half the things that are written about you! Then you have to go and defend your precious reputation in open court—*and you lose*!' he roared. 'Ginny, if you haven't been sleeping with every PR man in sight and any fake-tanned actor who's up for an Oscar, everyone else *thinks* you have—and that's crucifying me!'

'I know! I'm sorry! I really am!' she wailed.

Was that it? Had his pride been wounded because his wife was under suspicion? Ginny wondered if he'd had to defend her to his tough old grandfather, apologising for the dreadful publicity. And Leo *was* hurt. She could see that now; there was pain in his eyes and the lines that ran to the corners of his mouth.

Hesitantly she took a step or two forwards till she was an inch away from him. The depth of his anguish reached out to her heart and she longed to throw herself into his arms, to comfort him—herself too. To feel the strength of him encircling her, protecting her. Even a fighter had to take a rest and she'd been battling for too long.

'I hate that side of it!' she said fervently. 'You have to believe that—'

'But will you stop taking one assignment after another without giving yourself a decent break?' he demanded.

The question arrested her. Standing so close to him, her wan face uplifted, her famous tawny eyes wide with wonder, she knew that she wanted to. At that moment she'd had enough, and her job had evolved into a love-hate affair. But it had been her dream since she was tiny to be one of the top models in the world. She'd only just reached that status. Could she give it up and admit that she couldn't take the heat?

'I've never backed down. Never given up,' she explained slowly.

Although there was a brief softening of his bleak mouth, he made no reply to her comment. Her troubled eyes searched his. He was scowling, pushing back the dark lick of hair that flopped onto his forehead, and she felt a rush of deep affection at the familiar gesture.

Her long neck arched as she gracefully raised her arms and rested them lightly on his shoulders, which relaxed an inch, and she realised he'd been tensing, waiting for her decision. Hug me, she pleaded with her eyes.

But his arms remained at his sides, his fists clenched in anger. 'Do it. For me.'

Ginny's heart fluttered at the stark request. Knowing Leo as she did, it was obvious that he was too proud to beg. All he could do was issue orders. It made her soften with loving empathy, because he couldn't let go and neither could she. However much they had loved one another, there had always been a thin barrier between them, built by their childhood years of repression. And neither of them had ever dared to let their feelings fly.

But he had to understand what her life would be like without a career. 'Modelling is all I've ever known,' she whispered. The alternative horrified her, made her sick to the stomach, which was churning even now at the thought of abandoning her individuality and dedicating herself to the Brandon family's needs and expectations.

'I ask you again. Will you stop? It's killing you, Ginny,' he said gravely. 'I married a woman with more flesh on her bones. A woman who had time to dance in the moonlight on the daisy lawn.'

It had been the night of their engagement. She remembered that occasion with a deep ache in her heart. 'Oh, Leo!' she breathed helplessly. 'It can be like that again—' She stopped, overwhelmed, tears forming in her soft eyes.

At last, he reached for her. His arms came around her and she sank weakly against his beautiful body with a groan of relief. The magic was still there, she thought, resting her head on his shoulder, her mouth nuzzling his throat above the soft collar of his casual blue shirt.

'Can it, I wonder?' he murmured against her scalp.

The warmth of his words washed over her silky white-blonde hair and sent shivers down her back. The sensuality between them burned into her, tightening the skin on her body and melding them together. It had been so long. Months. Suddenly she needed him, needed the hard, physical release of sex.

'I know it can,' she whispered, kissing his throat. And she pressed her palm against his heart, giving a shudder of delight when she found that its beat was bumping erratically against her hand.

'When I married you,' he growled, breathing harshly into her ear, 'you were full of hopes for the future. Don't deny that we planned children—'

'That was before your family told me what obligations there were for the heir of Castlestowe! And...' She stifled a whimper of hunger. Leo's hand was slipping slowly down her slender back towards her hip. 'I—I

didn't know my career would take off so ferociously!'
she mumbled, trying to concentrate on her explanation.
'I had no idea I'd be jetting around the world.

'I feel tired of it all now,' she admitted. He didn't
know what she'd been through. Perhaps if she told him...
'Shortly before the trial,' she said, lifting her heart-
shaped face up to his, 'I did sixteen shows in six
days—'

'You didn't have to.' He wasn't looking at her. His
eyes were hooded again but she thought that they were
fixed on her cleavage, visible above the V of her jacket.
The cleavage was almost her signature. Unusual in a top
model, she had breasts. And the designers always provided her with clothes that featured them.

Leo had loved that once. He'd feasted his eyes on her
photographs and reached for her with a possessive
triumph because she was there, beside him, and she was
his wife. Who belonged to nobody but him. A shiver
ran through her body when she remembered how he'd
growled one night after making love to her, 'I'll kill any
man who takes you from me!'

She watched him lick his lips and warmth flooded her
loins. A feeling of devastating relief came with it because they would, could, *must* make up—now, before
the dreaded tea with Arabella.

'If I'd pulled out of the shows, I would have gone
mad, just sitting at home and thinking of the trial while
you were up at Castlestowe,' she said in a low and husky
voice. 'And everyone would have thought I was hiding
because I was guilty and ashamed. I had to brazen it
out, don't you see? OK, it wasn't easy. It half wrecked
me. I had early make-up calls and fittings every one of
those days. There were twenty-five TV crews backstage
at Dior for starters. But...'

Leo's firm hands pushed her back a little. 'But?' he asked with a frown.

'It was exciting—*is* exciting,' she admitted. 'My adrenaline runs when I'm working. Besides, I don't have a choice any more. I have to work if I'm to pay the legal costs. Being a wife and mother is a vocation,' she said gently. 'I want children, yes, but . . . not if it means living in remote Scotland with no neighbours for miles and miles. That's what you want, isn't it? Maybe when I'm older and I'm ready to settle down—'

'I feel so angry, Ginny.'

They were both breathing in a heavy rhythm. Her breasts rose and fell against his hard, lean chest. Grim-faced, he detached one hand and slid it between them, undoing the lowest pearl button.

Maybe this is the way, she thought hazily. They'd get close, be united again. Another button slid free. Control was slipping from her grasp. The need and the hunger for Leo—to share his body, to be comforted by its closeness—was overriding everything else.

'Give me a little time to earn the money for the costs,' she croaked as his hand brushed her naked skin beneath the jacket. Desire filled his face. Desire for her. With Leo, she could face anything. Debt, relentless, grinding hours of work, public shame—anything. 'I'll be less preoccupied from now on. It was only the terrible pressure of the trial that caused the problems between us,' she said, not too convincingly. 'Now that's over—'

'You'll be working twice as hard to keep bankruptcy at bay.' Leo appeared to be engrossed in the tantalisingly slow process of working the last cluster of pearls through the buttonhole. The jacket swung free, exposing the swell of her breasts. Leo's lips parted and he whispered in a slow breath of anticipation. 'Beautiful. I'd forgotten how beautiful.'

'Leo!' she breathed, filled with joy.

He reached out with a questing finger to stroke each half-hidden curve. She threw her head back and moaned, suspended in delight. It was a long time since she'd been touched. Her appetite had been suppressed and now it seemed insatiable.

'Ginny!' he muttered, his voice shaking with a barely controlled passion. It might have been anger or desire or despair. She couldn't tell. And she didn't care. All she wanted was to be held in his arms.

CHAPTER TWO

SLOWLY Leo reached out to draw the jacket from her shoulders. He held its soft folds halfway down her arms so that it acted like a strait-jacket. His avid eyes devoured her high, trembling breasts and suddenly she flinched, distressed by the mixture of anger and lust in the way he studied her.

'Love me,' Ginny begged.

'You want me to be your slave, like the others,' he said brutally.

'No! Don't do this to me, please, Leo—'

He let the jacket slip to the ground. She made to cover her nakedness with her hands, too stunned to think of running away. And there was something compelling about the way he looked at her, something that caught in her guts and twisted and speared her with an undeniable need. Her lashes lifted and she begged him for love with her huge tawny eyes.

'You want pity?' he muttered. 'Or are you acting as I've seen you act before, putting on a wistful face to dazzle your public? Hiding your real feelings...'

'No,' she whispered, shaking her head. It was heavy. Her whole body felt lethargic and languid. But he wanted sex, and anger drove him, not affection. 'You know I find it hard to let go, that it takes me a while before...'

She gasped. His arm had drawn her to him. Deliberately he moved her body against his, lightly, tantalisingly, with the finesse of a master with years of experience. The softness of his shirt brushed her nipples and he groaned, giving them a delicate squeeze between his finger and thumb. Just enough to sharpen her hunger, to send needles of desire bursting into each breast. She heard herself moan, felt her pelvis contract and hated herself for being so easily controlled.

'What are you?' murmured Leo. 'Who are you? Witch or angel? A false, heartless woman with an ego larger than Napoleon's, or perhaps—'

'I'm no angel. But I'm innocent,' she protested, reeling under the torment of his fingers. Her breasts felt tight and hot, the flesh glowing for him. Beneath her frantic hands, his shirt moved over his satin skin and she had to force herself not to rip the buttons open and lay her mouth on his breast. Now she had to keep her head and defend herself all over again. To her husband. Or lose him for ever.

Taking a deep breath, she said jerkily, 'I—I warned you when we married that the media would tell l-lies about me and...'

She lost the thread of her sentence. Her head turned from side to side in pleasure as Leo forced his thigh between her long, silk-clad legs and she couldn't resist making a small, squirming movement because it might help to hold her need till she'd explained. And then, she thought hazily, they could make love freely, without hate and suspicion.

'Oh, Leo!' she whispered, knowing what he was going to do.

His hands were sliding down her hips. They reached the edge of her skirt and slowly, watching her, his velvety gaze flicking from her softly parted lips to her drowsy eyes, he wriggled it up till it was around her waist. Now there was only silk between her hot hunger and his linen-clad knee.

Leo's jaw tightened when he looked down at the length of her exposed legs. Black Lacroix stockings topped with a deep band of Calais lace. Dove-grey satin briefs. 'Hell!' he growled thickly. 'How could any man not be tempted by you?'

'I—I freeze them off,' she rasped, incapable of breathing steadily.

'Irresistible,' he said, smouldering grey eyes and brutally tentative fingers hypnotised by the gap above her stocking-tops.

Her pelvis pushed forward a little in demand before she could stop the movement and he smiled in triumph. Ginny closed her eyes in despair because he still didn't believe that she had been faithful to him. His mouth brushed hers, making her tremble. His palms rotated on her nipples, warm, merciless, till they thrust in shameful dark peaks, elongating painfully, begging for the moistness of his mouth.

Panting, driven crazy, she abandoned all restraint and began to unpick his buttons, feverishly fumbling with them as if she were drunk. 'Make love to me,' she said urgently, lifting her beautiful, flawless face.

Leo's mouth hovered a millimetre above hers. 'You are the most desirable woman in the world,' he husked. 'Envied by millions, coveted by millions.' Something dark came into his expression. 'However, for the time being,' he whispered into her parted lips, their breath mingling, 'you can consider yourself exclusively mine.'

She wanted to be exclusively his for hours. Leo prided himself on long, sensual lovemaking sessions. Unconsciously, she gave a luxurious stretch of her body. 'Yes,' she moaned. 'Yes, please, Leo.'

'I've wanted to make love to you since the moment you walked in. I'm more than ready.' He took her hand

and placed it on his groin. She groaned to feel him so hard, to feel the leap of heat against her trembling fingers.

'Leo,' she whispered. 'Make love to me properly. Long and slow. As you used to. Please, darling. Please.'

Desperate to persuade him, she stood on tiptoe and slid her hands to his head, pressing it down and kissing him with all her heart and soul. With a wriggle of her hips, she gyrated on the thigh that was thrust between her legs and moved her breasts across his chest—partly to assuage her own demands and partly to entice him to indulge in hours of pleasure with her.

'Witch!' he growled throatily. His hands ran down her body possessively. 'I don't know whether to hate you or despise you or—'

'Love me,' she whispered, twining her fingers in his hair. 'Please, Leo. Love me.'

With a muttered groan that came from deep inside him, he bore her down to the polished wood floor as if he could no longer bear to hold back, stretching her arms over her head and covering her with his hard body. She felt his mouth on hers, fierce and uncompromising, angry, perhaps, because he wanted her so badly when he thought that she was worthless as a wife. And at the back of her mind she prayed that their lovemaking *would* bring them close, that the anger would subside and they could start to unravel the tangled threads of their unstitched marriage.

The onslaught of his mouth, teeth, tongue and hands and her frantic attempts to ease her despair with physical energy alone caused them to tumble and roll across the floor, her back sliding on the slippery wood, and Ginny became swamped in a whirl of sensation—the feel of silkwood and the smell of polish on her naked back, the pressure of Leo's muscular arms around her and the wonderful sweetness of his mouth, tugging gently at her breast.

Lost in deep passion and an uncontrollable hunger, grabbing, clutching, kissing, they slid into a table. Something crashed to the floor—a lamp, an ornament; she wasn't sure what—but Leo ignored everything, intent on possessing her, sweetly caressing every inch of her body as if to drive away any memory she might have of other men.

Equally driven, she gave up trying to undo his buttons and pulled the edges of his shirt with both hands, burying her face in his chest. She wanted him naked, to feel his body against hers, because only then would she dare to believe that they could shut out the threat from all outsiders and prove to one another that they were still in love.

He was as helpless, as frantic as she. Finally his naked body met hers and she let out a long, loud groan of relief. At last he was inside her, stroking her with a fiercely restrained gentleness. Overjoyed, she forced her eyes to flutter open, her lush mouth smiling with pleasure. Ginny arched her body in demand. 'Love me.'

Her mouth teased his, urging it to soften into a sensual curve. And because she wanted him to desire her more than ever and to remember this moment for a long, long time she used all the arts she'd ever learnt from him, writhing sinuously, clutching his buttocks and thus increasing his unbearably slow and deliberate thrust.

She wanted to make him desperate for her. To love her—*her*. With a siren's lure in her eyes, she slid her tongue out and licked the sweat over the curving arcs of his chest, teasing the nipples till he gave a satisfying groan and she felt his rhythm increase to a pitch where she couldn't think any more, was only capable now of reacting like an animal, wildly driving her body against his, countering his thrust with equally hard, demanding jerks of her own body, drawing in her pelvis to hold him tighter and devouring him with her mouth as he devoured her, as if they'd starved for months and wanted to fill themselves to satiation.

Ginny flung her arms around Leo violently, bearing him over in a wild and uncontrollable tumble that had them both fighting to hold their bodies linked and to maintain the beautiful, shuddering rhythm, while she emptied all her passion into her body, kissing Leo with a fervour born of desperation and urgency.

He was so strong, so beautiful. They had been so in love and she wanted that back—the wonderful moments they'd shared together, the quiet evenings by the firelight, the walks in the park. A groan broke from her parted lips and she bit into his shoulder to stem her distress that their love had been threatened. He gasped and kissed her so hard that she felt the deep pressure of his teeth on her lips.

And then her body began to sing as it had never sung before, every nerve taut and stretched, all the bitter-sweet pain rising with the crescendo of Leo's fierce movement, the beautiful satin strength within her offering the wonderful promise of a release from all her distress and tension.

'Ginny,' he rasped thickly into her hair. 'Ginny, Ginny!'

She sobbed, groaned loudly, not caring who heard—oblivious of everything but the sensations crawling through her, the tingling, rippling waves driving all conscious thought away, lifting her into a fevered delight that shuddered for a few seconds on a peak of ecstasy and held there, seemingly for ever, while their bodies remained like tensile steel, taut and rigid, only their pulses and hearts and their blood pounding, and everything focused on the lyrical thrust of their loins and the spinning spirals of pagan pleasure that was driving them slowly insane with exquisitely agonising sensation.

And when she thought she'd die of love Leo let out a deep, shuddering groan. The turmoil that had held her in its thrall slowly subsided, easing with it every muscle in her body.

Beneath him, crushed by him as he lay for a moment in exhaustion—yet still somehow tense—she felt limp and drained. But her face shone with a radiant joy that came from every inch of her body, her heart, her soul. 'Oh, Leo!' she mumbled incoherently, blinded by happy tears.

And then he groaned. Once, twice, as if in despair.

His welcome weight lifted away when she wanted him to stay and to hold her in his arms. Her naked body chilled with the emptiness that was left by his absence. Dazed and confused, she struggled to lift her lids and clear her vision. Her heart missed a beat. Sounds nearby told her that he was dressing.

'Leo?' she murmured weakly. Even from there she could hear his harsh breathing, rasping like an angry saw. Panic clutched her heart. No, she thought. They were bonded together for ever now...

'Yes?'

She whimpered at the curtly spoken word. 'Didn't you...wasn't it...good?' she asked tentatively.

'Stunningly good. Highly accomplished and extremely satisfying,' he husked, the words shooting out painfully. His eyes smouldered at her. 'What a lot you've learnt since we last made love!'

'Don't *say* that!' Unusually awkward and uncoordinated, she struggled in horror to a sitting position and watched him grimly wrench his trousers up to his waist. 'Not so, Leo! I—'

'Don't try to explain,' he growled, angrily snapping his shirt around his sweat-licked torso. Every movement tight with anger, he picked up his shoes and began to stalk to the door. Ginny had the impression that he'd turn on her like a wounded animal and savage her if he stayed. 'Quite a sexual artiste, aren't you, now someone's taught you how to be uninhibited?'

'No one taught me,' she breathed, her throat dry with fear.

His eyes chilled every inch of her body as his scorn-filled gaze swept over it and dismissed her denial with a snort of disbelief. 'You expect me to believe that, after your performance just now? Yes, it was "good". For a moment there you made me forget everything. We were lovers again—but lovers as we'd never been before. And then I realised that some other man—or men—must have been teaching you the art of love.'

'No!' she wailed.

'I wish I could believe you!' he said fervently. '*I* wanted to be that man, Ginny! *I* wanted you to unfold that tight rein you kept on yourself. But no, some jerk I don't even know has shown you how to gain access to your sexual well!' He drew in a deep, shuddering breath, his face bleak with the same dark hell that he was digging for her. 'How could you, Ginny?' he roared. 'How could you do it? That exhibition told me everything I needed to know. Thanks for the information. Now I'm under no illusions about you.'

Ginny covered her icy, trembling body as well as she could with her hands. 'Leo—' she husked.

'Save it!' he said curtly over his shoulder. Then he turned, his face as black as thunder. 'I want honesty in my wife,' he bit out. 'Decency. A woman I can respect. Not a painted doll who uses her beauty to get what she wants. You did that with me just now, didn't you?'

'I—I wanted you to...care for me, to help me,' she jerked out.

'Sure. You let me have you because you wanted something,' he said, his mouth curling in contempt. 'Now I *do* believe the stories about you.'

Dispassionately, he studied her for long, interminable seconds while she fought the tears and her total exhaustion. She had to get up, run to him, *love* him into realising that everyone had misunderstood her and put her into a mould of their own making, not hers.

'I am innocent, Leo,' she said, wondering if she could ever crack that icy regard, the look of hauteur which reminded her forcibly that he was The Honourable Leo Brandon, born and bred with pride.

'Like hell! I should have seen it coming. I can't entirely blame you. That's the kind of world you entered when you were too young to prevent your slow corruption. I know what goes on, Ginny. But we Brandons prefer to protect the honour of our wives, if only to keep the blood line pure. You're right. Our worlds don't mix. Pack your things. You've got an hour to be out of here. Leave nothing behind to remind me of a very bad mistake I made. We're finished, Ginny. I'm divorcing you.'

A harsh, guttural wail ripped out from deep inside her. But he'd gone, in a storming, door-slamming rush. Ginny slowly lifted her head, tilting it back, and closed her eyes in despair. Her white-blonde hair swept down her naked back and she registered that the tightly secured chignon had been dismantled by Leo's hands, by his wild lovemaking. She blushed, at a loss to understand quite how a strictly brought-up woman could have abandoned herself so completely to the devils within her.

No wonder he'd been shocked. She was too, merely thinking of what they'd done, red stains working their way up from her slender feet to her mortified face. So she'd ruined her chance to show Leo that they could be lovers again by revealing an untamed and uncontrolled side of herself that he must have hated.

After all, she thought mournfully, everyone adored her Grace Kelly manner. They loved her serenity, her calmness. Leo had said that he liked the fact that she always behaved like a lady. Some lady. But that was what he'd wanted—a woman who'd project an image of breeding. And now she'd ruined that.

Her body quivered with the pleasure that had rippled through it in great roller-coaster waves. Over and over again they'd crashed through her and physically she felt totally sated. Emotionally, however...

Her perfect white teeth snagged her lower lip. It was bruised and swollen and she touched it with her finger, wondering whether Leo had always known what real, uninhibited sex was like and if she'd been a disappointment to him before because she'd never given her whole self. Till it was too late.

But he'd wanted her. Desperately. Beyond all his rigidly imposed self-control. He'd been crazy to have her and he'd hated her for that because he would have preferred to take her with cool ruthlessness and fling her aside.

Perhaps she could build on his desire. A ragged breath shuddered through her and she stood, quickly dressing. It was the only hope she had. Hastily she searched for enough of the scattered hairpins to do her chignon again and had to give up, combing the silken hair with her fingers instead. She paused as Leo's words came back to her, jolting her with their intensity.

Divorce... Life without Leo. Cold horror iced her body. He was all she had! The only man she'd ever loved. She wouldn't, mustn't lose him! Especially now that she'd given her whole self to him, abandoning a lifetime of restraint to show him what he meant to her.

Frantically she ran out of the library and began to search the rooms downstairs, then hitched up her tight skirt and raced up the wide stairs two at a time.

Relief flooded through her when she heard the shower running in their *en suite* bathroom. Thinking of nothing else but convincing him, she went straight to the cabinet, opened the door and walked inside.

'Leo! Listen to me!' she begged, water plastering her hair to her scalp.

'What the—? You're fully clothed, Ginny! Get out!' he said with an irritable frown.

But she held him, her arms wrapped around his waist. And instantly he became aroused. Relief burst into her mind. She had a chance. 'Don't turn me away, Leo,' she said softly, lifting her face to his. 'I can't imagine life without you—'

'You're already living it without me,' he muttered, wrenching her arms away and flinging open the shower door.

She stood there, saturated, dazed. Don't give up hope. Try again, she told herself. Try again. Stripping off her jacket as she spoke, she said, 'Everything is good except for the problem of my work and Castlestowe. We can discuss our differences and compromise. Change things—'

'One thing's changed. You've become a spectacular lay,' he said crudely. 'But I don't want a tramp for a wife or for the mother of my child.'

'I'm not a tramp,' she insisted quietly.

'The stories—'

'Are only stories. They're not true,' she cried desperately, easing off her soaking skirt.

'I've heard the details.' His eyes flashed. 'Confirmed by several people—'

'They're repeating the same lie that someone's circulated!' she cried, beginning to fear that her protestations would be in vain. 'I can't prove my fidelity, Leo! But surely you must give me the benefit of the doubt?'

The lines around his aristocratic mouth were deep with pain. 'How can I when you so brilliantly display a sexual expertise you never had before? When you respond to me with such devastating sensuality that I—? Oh, Ginny!' He threw his head back in a gesture of helplessness. 'I stood up for you. I looked everyone straight in the eye at my club when they whispered behind my back. But now I'm sure I'm a cuckold. And I sure as hell won't stand for that!' he snapped. 'I want a divorce. I must remarry. Time is running out—my grandfather is ninety. I would like him to see that I have an heir to the earldom before he dies.'

'Leo! Is that more important than our marriage?' she faltered, naked now and grabbing a thick towelling robe and slipping into it.

'Having a child is an important part of marriage for me,' he growled. 'It always has been. That—and having a loyal wife.'

Ginny's anguished eyes watched him stride to the mahogany linen press. French. Priceless. Louis the something, she remembered, and inherited with a castle full of French furniture after one of the earls had married into the French aristocracy in the eighteenth century. France and Scotland had always been linked in the past. She thought of the castle, sitting on the windswept crag, all turrets and drawbridges, narrow windows and vast, draughty halls, and shivered.

It was an inheritance she didn't understand and didn't want to be part of. It had been a mistake for them to marry. She'd been naïve to imagine that their marriage could be ordinary. Leo had expectations she couldn't meet however much she loved him.

'I love you,' she said quietly, sadly.

He froze, his arm halted in the action of reaching for a clean shirt. It was a moment before he moved or spoke again. 'I'm not sure you do,' he said shortly, slipping his arms into the shirt and not looking at her. 'Love has little to do with it, anyway. We're incompatible and that's that.' He picked up the cuff-links that she knew had been given to his father by a minor royal and finally met her eyes. As he dressed, she thought mournfully, he looked more and more the perfect gentleman with every impeccable garment he put on.

'I have a duty to continue the family line,' he continued. 'To see the Brandon name die out after nearly a thousand uninterrupted years would be unthinkable. I had hoped to father children by a woman I loved but it seems I'm to be denied that.'

Ginny's eyes widened. 'Are you intending to make a marriage of convenience?' she cried.

His eyes stared sightlessly ahead and he was still for several seconds before he answered. 'Do I have any option? Love was always a risk for both of us. We didn't know much about it from our parents, did we? And now all I have left is Castlestowe and a dynastic marriage some time in the future.'

She couldn't believe her ears. He'd marry, make love to a woman and father children all for the sake of a wretched blood-line... 'No! I won't give you up to anyone else!' she seethed.

'No?' He wouldn't look at her and his face was grim, his mouth working as if he was grinding his teeth. 'We'll see about that.' With a look of sheer determination on his face, he picked up a pair of linen trousers and stalked into his dressing room, locking the door behind him.

Two years and a few months or so later Ginny was secretly divorced.

Leo had convinced her that he had washed his hands of her only eight hours after the incident in the shower.

She'd been tucked up on the big window-seat in a guest bedroom, horrible racking sobs tearing at her body, when she'd heard a racket in their bedroom. Laughter—squeals of it, and Leo's chuckle. She'd been stunned for a moment, then had stormed in, to find him and Arabella, naked in the huge four-poster bed, romping like eager children. Their bedroom. Their bed. Even now, after two interminable, depressing years, it made her ball her fists in fury.

At the time the shock had driven her out, screaming hysterically, fleeing to the nearest room and locking herself in. And she'd cried rivers of tears till exhaustion had brought sleep where she lay, poignantly, cruelly, on the bed in the nursery where there would be no child of hers now. The irony hadn't been lost on her in the morning when she'd woken.

In a surprising act of generosity, Leo had agreed to keep their divorce a secret from everyone but his family and Chas for a while. It had meant that she wasn't hassled by the Press. The lawyers had been paid well to ensure their secrecy and the divorce had been handled in a small market town where the sleepy court reporter had failed to recognise the woman called Virginia Brandon as Ginny McKenzie.

But then she'd been wearing a Paisley headscarf, an old trench coat and enormous spectacles. And Leo had turned up in a checked cap and an anorak. They'd nodded coldly and hadn't even laughed at one another's strange attire. Laughter hadn't been something she'd expected to feature much in her life for a while. Her life had been shattered and the only thing she'd felt was cold—a stillness of her body as if the warm blood in her veins had turned to a trickle of ice. And she'd wondered if she'd ever be warm again.

The divorce had been alarmingly quick and straightforward. The lawyers had assured the judge that neither of them wanted or needed maintenance and that was that. Her marriage was at an end.

Despite closing down her emotions after the divorce, despite working every waking hour so that she could forget Leo and maintain her position in the modelling hierarchy and pay back her debt, she'd still felt raw inside. Every day she'd ached for Leo and wished that they could be together because her heart was breaking in the most painful way—slowly dying from disuse.

But she'd never shown those feelings to anyone. Look where it had got her when she'd flung her heart and soul into loving her husband! Ex-husband, she'd continually corrected herself, gritting her teeth with the pain of a chapter in her life that was now ended.

And how much had the humiliation of being rejected damaged her self-confidence? It had taken her a long

time to smooth over the nerves she'd felt when facing
the public. Hours of almost maniacal preparation, so
that her face had been a perfect mask and every gesture
had been rehearsed.

Only then had she been able to bear to confront
everyone, knowing that they were whispering, gos-
siping, wondering about the 'perfect lady' who'd turned
out to be a tigress in a variety of beds. Head held high,
she'd coolly met their eyes with a challenge and they'd
always looked away first.

But she'd become lonely, trusting no one but Chas,
who rarely left her side and had become father and
brother and friend to her. And now she was truly alone
because even Chas didn't quite know what was in her
heart: an ache for the man she couldn't have because
they couldn't live together, their lives having veered away
from each other too dramatically ever to meet and link
again.

Emerging from Heathrow with Chas and turning the key
in her coupé parked in the long-term car park, Ginny
suddenly wanted privacy. Divorced, theoretically free but
forever a prisoner of Leo's magnetism, she smiled faintly
at Chas.

'I'd like to drive myself. Just this once. Would you
take a taxi?'

And, driving through the streets of London to her flat
in Chelsea, she grimly steeled every bone in her body
and held back the tears that had threatened from the
moment her solicitor had telephoned her while she was
in Paris to say that her decree absolute had come
through.

Suddenly she had wanted to be home—and alone with
her memories. She'd cancelled everything in her diary,

saying that she felt ill. It was the first time she'd ducked her obligations.

Her marriage was dead and buried. Might as well face up to that, she thought. Her lip quivered and she bit it for daring to betray her.

'Oh!' she mumbled unhappily, driving into the mews and bumping over the cobbles to the far end. 'I hate him! I hate him!' And she wished it weren't a lie.

There came the slam of a taxi door and Chas appeared by her window. 'Want a shoulder?' he offered casually.

Ginny shook her head, too upset to speak. She reached out her hand to temper the refusal and withdrew it after Chas's brief pat. 'I'm doing a Garbo,' she said huskily. 'Come in. But I'd like to be alone. I feel I've come to the end of an era. I need to plan the next.' She managed a smile but it was feeble.

'Sure. You must be tired. You've been going like the clappers. Glad you're taking a break. I'll keep everyone at bay.'

Thankful for his tact, Ginny flicked the remote control to open the doors and drove into the garage, leaving all her things in the car to collect later. On entering the flat, she absently picked up the mail on the mat and wandered into the kitchen to make some tea, shrugging off the elegant Ralph Lauren jacket in the soft shade of blue that...

She frowned. That Leo had loved. He would like this, she thought mournfully, indulging in self-pity for a few seconds. The flowing palazzo pants caressed her thighs, hinting at her slenderness, her flat, taut stomach. The sand-coloured camisole drifted elegantly over her breasts to the cinched-in waist. There was no one to appreciate the way she looked now.

She briskly put a stop to this line of thought and got out the tea-things. The healing brew, she thought wryly. When she really needed healing arms around her.

If only she'd been brought up by her real parents! she sighed, curling up in an old comfy chair while the kettle boiled. If so, there might have been a friendly cuddle for her now.

Ginny sighed wistfully. It was so sad that her own mother had been unable to care for her. Her mother had developed a serious phobia about cleanliness which had meant that when Ginny was born her mother had become hysterical at all the mess a baby brought. Or so the McKenzies, her adoptive parents, had told her. They would never reveal her mother's whereabouts and Ginny was wary of discovering that her mother cared nothing for her.

Sarah Temple. That was all she knew of her mother— besides a few memories, dim but unpleasant. Vague recollections of being held grimly to a starched apron-front, a woman screaming, and a feeling of terrified guilt at the mess she'd made once when she'd had a tummy upset. Had her mother cried on and on for hours, or was that a faulty memory?

She thought with compassion of what must have been a tense, uptight woman who'd apparently been eager to give her away when she was four to a strict Scottish couple.

The McKenzies were well off. Andrew was a respected politician. That was how she'd met Leo—their fathers were both in politics and she'd reluctantly gone along with her adoptive parents to a country weekend at Castlestowe when she was nearly eighteen. Hated it. Loved Leo. Fool.

Hadn't she seen the different worlds they moved in? Butlers, maids, cut-glass crystal, banners of long-forgotten battles and grim oil paintings of even grimmer ancestors?

Ginny wearily uncoiled her long, long legs from the chair and made the tea, carrying a mug in to Chas.

'I've got some thinking to do,' she told him, her face wan and strained. 'I'll be in the study. Use the TV in the drawing room if you want. It won't bother me. And would you lock up later? I'll probably be pacing the floor for a while. I have to get my head together. You understand?' she asked in a hesitant plea.

'Sure, Ginny,' he said gently. 'Let me know if you want anything. I'm here and I've got waterproof skin if necessary.'

Her pathetic attempt at a smile quivered on her lips and then she turned, almost broken by the tenderness of his expression. Because she had wanted Leo to look like that. And he hadn't given a damn.

Despairing, she tucked herself in the little office, fixed with all the latest technology to enable her to keep in contact with designers and agents around the world. Everyone seemed to be doing things for her. Few were, in reality.

Ginny switched on the answering machine and half-heartedly listened to the messages. Business. Nothing personal or affectionate. And suddenly she was filled with an overwhelming feeling of need. If only she knew who her father was! The McKenzies had refused to speak of her mother's situation and Ginny had no idea whether she was illegitimate or if her real father had died early on in her life.

Maybe she should ring up the McKenzies and ask. But, knowing what their opinion of her morals would be, she shrank from doing so. They'd never speak to her, never acknowledge that they had anything to do with her.

It was up to her to take hold of her life. To make it her own again. Maybe she'd find happiness. Her mouth turned down in a grimace. It would make a change.

As a child she'd been hated. Thin as a rake, stuttering, bullied every day, she'd spent her school days in constant fear of having her head stuck in the lavatory bowl, or being ambushed on the way home and having to explain her torn and dirty clothes to the perfectionist Ada McKenzie.

She smiled ruefully, remembering how she'd vowed to show those vicious schoolgirls that she was *somebody*!

And, strangely, it had been Ada McKenzie who'd given her the way out. Because Ginny had kept dropping things in her clumsy, nervous state, she had been sent to a ruthless ballet mistress who'd taught her grace and control. She'd learnt how to walk and project serenity, composure and elegance. Her eyes had been set on the stars from then on.

Although boys hadn't dated her because she'd towered over them—and had been too skinny in their eyes—she had been discovered and swept into the world of modelling in her mid-teens, suddenly to be dazzled by the power she had over her own life at last. Or had she?

Her fingers idly turned over the letters, already opened by the agency which vetted her mail. Paris, New York, Milan... the usual. She flung them to one side and picked up a newspaper. It was a while before she realised that it was a couple of months old. In the act of putting it down, she saw her own name. Her real name. Intrigued, she read the advert in the 'Personal' column.

Virginia Temple. Born 26.8.71, Sunnyside Nursing Home, Glasgow, subsequently 47 Barracks Lane. Last heard of at Lee Lane Women's Refuge, 1975, in the care of Sarah Temple.

Please contact the office below where you will learn something to your advantage.

How odd! Excitement began to make her breathe faster. Sarah Temple! Her mother! Perhaps this would lead her to her mother! The end of her pencil was stabbing at the numbers and she was blurting out who she was.

'I'm Jack Lacey, acting on behalf of Monsieur St Honoré,' said the solicitor. 'My client wishes to talk to you. I can vouch for him. He's absolutely above board—but I must tell you that you're not the first to answer St Honoré's advert. Still, you have a right to go. I have airline tickets for you to St Lucia. And accommodation is included.'

'St Lucia? Why?' she asked eagerly. 'Is this about my mother's whereabouts?'

'Could be,' said Lacey guardedly. 'Monsieur St Honoré has been searching for his daughter for some time—'

'My father?' A warmth wound its way through Ginny's cold heart. Her father. 'My *father*! I don't believe it! Hold on!' she said excitedly.

Cradling her mobile phone, she punched out the numbers of her travel agency and upgraded the ticket to first class, then changed her mind and decided to travel steerage. On this trip she would be an ordinary passenger.

'Maybe *not* your father,' said the solicitor with a solicitor's caution as she carried on two conversations at the same time. 'Someone else went out a while ago—a

young woman born in the same nursing home as you—
but I've heard nothing from her so I'm assuming she
wasn't St Honoré's daughter after all.'

'Maybe I am!' she breathed. 'It would be wonderful!
Tell him I'm coming. How do I contact him?'

'You don't. I can give you no information—his in-
structions, my dear, and I'm afraid I've let on too much
as it is. He's wary of imposters, wary of being fleeced.
Go out there. He'll contact *you*.'

'I'm on the next plane,' she cried, feeling as if she
could get there without one at all! 'I want to find my
family,' she said wistfully.

It would give her someone of her own to love. Her
face was suffused with joy at the thought. Even if St
Honoré proved not to be her father, the advert suggested that he knew something about her background.
And that might lead her to finding out more about her
parents.

In any case, this was what she needed right now because she adored St Lucia. And it was somewhere warm.
A place to lie and think. To iron out her life. Maybe
just for a rest, before she fell into the hurly-burly of
running herself ragged every day to finish paying back
what she owed to the courts.

Her brow furrowed. There were dangers, of course.
Whatever Jack Lacey said, this man could be a kook
like the ones whose letters were now held back from her
by the agency to save her any worry.

Yet the pleasure of travelling without an entourage
appealed; the idea of being able to shape her life instead
of running behind everyone else who was organising it
for her was suddenly the most desirable thing in the
world. Perhaps in a foreign place, on an island she'd
worked on before and had loved, she could let herself

cry without worrying that photographers might record her misery and splash it all over the features pages.

Almost excitedly she ran to Chas to tell him that he had a few weeks' holiday starting *now* instead of in ten days' time when his wife was due to have her baby. But something stopped her from mentioning that she was going to see a man who might be her father. Saying that out loud would be tempting fate to disappoint her.

And she couldn't take any more knocks. She was too fragile. One more disappointment could tip her over the edge.

CHAPTER THREE

KNOWING the island roads as she did, Ginny wisely took the helicopter ride from the airport. It set her down in the delightful small town of Soufrière.

Slipping off her winter layers down to her sleeveless body and swirling jade-green silk skirt, she twisted a matching scarf through her newly cut hair—now in a page-boy bob—and hoped that the new hairstyle plus the enormous sunglasses and a conscious effort on her part not to project glamour would hide her identity. So far no one had rushed up to her, pointed, sniggered or trained cameras on her. Wonderful. Freedom! And she was smiling naturally for the first time in ages.

A small dugout with an outboard motor ferried her to the hotel, speeding along at an exhilarating rate over the smooth, glassy sea. When she saw the bay she fell in love with it at first sight.

It was a place that she'd always meant to visit but had never found time for in the hectic schedule of being photographed for magazine covers. Anse La Verdure Hotel sat halfway up a jungly hill, only partly visible among the tropical trees. Coconut palms backed the gentle curve of the beach and boats bobbed in the bay. The beauty and peace of the isolated cove offered all the privacy she could desire.

Leaving Reception to call her if Monsieur St Honoré arrived, she walked up the hill to her villa, her heart lifting at the glorious view that unfolded when she entered.

The two-bedroomed cantilevered villa sprawled out over the hill and was open to the fresh air on three sides. Its skilful design afforded total privacy, yet gave maximum exposure to the glorious blue skies and rampant vegetation.

For three days she never left the room or the big sun-deck, waiting for the call from St Honoré. She didn't even think. All she did was read the novels she'd bought at the airport.

Already she was rested. On the fourth morning she woke late and decided to trace St Honoré herself. Stripping off her satin nightdress, ignoring the clothes she'd shed last night in deliciously teenagerish chaos all over the floor, she walked into the shower, laughing at the birds which flew in and prinked their feathers where the water splashed on the tiles.

It would be paradise if only Leo could be with her too. She sighed. Leo would be the only man in her heart for the rest of her life. She loved him so deeply that she would carry her love to the grave. And dreamily she imagined his face, his body, his wonderful smile, wondering how she could resurrect his love for her.

Her reverie was interrupted by a banging on the door. 'Oh, drat!' she sighed, reaching for her robe. 'Yes?' she asked warily, when she opened the door.

'My name is St Honoré,' began the unshaven and dishevelled flaxen-haired male with incredibly piercing blue eyes. 'I wish to God it wasn't, but I imagine you're pleased.'

'Oh!' she said, startled. 'Yes, I am!'

He wore only a pair of shorts, was tanned to the colour of teak—and seemed as furious as hell. And he obviously was far too young—perhaps thirtyish?—to be her father. The disappointment swept through her and she realised that she'd set more store by this meeting than she'd thought.

'Let's talk,' he said tightly in an oddly accented voice. Sexy French crossed with the lovely Caribbean sing-song. Though, with a name like his, he probably had French ancestry.

She drew her robe firmly about her body. 'I'd like that—' she began politely.

'Fine.' Before she knew what he was doing, he'd walked past her and up the stairs into the room. When she padded uncertainly after him, he whirled round and frowned. 'Are you here for the old man's money?'

Ginny blinked and understood. 'You mean your father?' she hazarded, and remembered the promise that she'd learn something to her advantage. Her heart thudded. She was fair, like him. Could they be related? Brother and sister? 'I could be—'

'If you've come to play gold-digger, then I'd advise you to go home,' he told her curtly, 'before you're in deep, deep trouble!'

Her eyes narrowed at his animosity. 'I've only just arrived!' she said spiritedly.

'I want to know what your expectations are,' he muttered.

He began to walk towards her and she retreated till her back was against a pillar. His hands came up and she wriggled, mortified that her action had wrenched the robe open a little.

Just as he laid his hands on her naked shoulders, she heard a gasp and both she and St Honoré jerked their heads around in unison. Ginny's eyes widened in shock. A beautiful and clearly distressed woman with heavily tumbled brown hair was staring at them in blank horror amid the chaos of Ginny's scattered clothing. The woman cried 'Pascal!' twice and fainted dead away, crumpling in a heap on the floor.

The grip on Ginny's arms was released. Without a word, the man—Pascal, presumably—ran to the woman, picked her up and carried her out.

The peace, the serenity and her sense of calm had been shattered. Ginny clung to the veranda post, her chest heaving, her hair falling about her face. The woman was obviously Pascal St Honoré's wife, lover or partner. Ginny went scarlet, thinking back to how it must have looked to an outsider—she with her robe falling open, thrust against the pillar with Pascal's hands holding her, his face close to hers, urgent and intense. An intensity that could have been interpreted as sexual passion.

'Oh, *no*!' she whispered hopelessly. 'More scandal. More accusations.'

And she groaned when she heard footsteps on the wooden stairs that led up from the front door to her room, dreading the prospect of the woman's disgust when she accused her of seducing her guy.

But before she could move she heard a voice that froze her where she stood.

'Often entertain half-naked men, do you?' drawled Leo's voice.

Ice formed inside her. She seemed to have been frozen right through by those soft, sinister tones. Leo! His contempt had rung out across the room, hurting her with a sharpness that rendered her temporarily mute.

Then the two years of killing all outward emotion concerning Leo came into play and she turned, cool and haughty, mistress of herself despite the shaking of her legs and the sickness in her stomach.

She let her eyes wander up and down him, calculating the amount of insult that she could get away with safely. It was nearly her undoing.

Scornful and hard he might look, but he was also flinging his wretched masculine appeal at her and she burned beneath his slow scrutiny of her barely covered body.

'Surely my behaviour is no concern of yours?' she said mildly, tying up her gaping robe and somehow wandering with a deceptive casualness across to the stagey dressing table.

'It is when you involve what appears to be a distressed wife in full flight,' he said coldly. 'You are a little tramp, Virginia!'

Virginia, she thought dully. Formal. Detached. Only her adoptive parents had ever called her that. 'For men it's all right, is it?' she asked in a low tone, racked with pain as she remembered the horrific sight of Arabella and Leo in bed together. Her voice hardened. 'It didn't matter that you entertained a naked woman in our bed or that *I* was a distressed woman in full flight?'

'You deserved what you got,' he said brutally. 'I doubt if that unhappy little innocent did!'

'It wasn't what it seemed!' she defended. 'He'll explain to his wife, if that's who she is.'

'If she believes you two were doing something innocuous, she's more guileless than she looks,' snapped Leo.

She quivered involuntarily. What was it about him? Her eyes lingered on his mouth. A hardness, a predatory sensuality. She felt her stomach lurch. He was somehow dangerous—not the man she'd known before. And that excited her, against her will.

'I hope she does believe it was a misunderstanding on her husband's part, because it's true,' she said huskily, certain that Pascal would placate his wife by explaining the possible relationship between himself and the half-naked woman he'd been accosting.

And, worrying that her senses were spilling into her brains, she sat down on the stool and smiled coolly, non-committally at Leo's reflection in the mirror while she unhooked the hair-dryer.

Her hand wavered, however, because she suddenly remembered the mind-blowing sex with him on the library floor... as she had remembered it so many times since. And every time it had left a raw ache inside her. This time he was here in person and it was worse. Because she still loved him and he'd cheated on her. Even now she wanted to scream at him and ease her impotent anger. Yet she knew that she had to keep calm and dignified for her own sake.

Obviously irritated by the noise, he took the hair-dryer from her hand and replaced it. With a deep sigh, she angled her head to show her exasperation and asked coolly, 'Why are you here—and how did you find me?'

'Chas,' he drawled, his fingers resting on the nape of her neck.

'How could he?' she protested resentfully.

Slowly Leo's hands ran up through her wet hair and she was reminded of another time, another lifetime, when she'd been so desperate to hold her marriage together, to keep Leo's love, that she'd walked into the shower fully dressed. And been rebuffed. Her heart hardened.

'I rang you,' he said casually, 'to make sure you knew the divorce had gone through. Chas didn't mean to betray you. He accidentally mentioned that you were in St Lucia and I tricked him into giving away a little more.

A name—St Honoré.' A sinister note had crept into his voice.

'So?' She shook her head to rid herself of his unwanted caress. Well, she admitted to herself, it *was* wanted, but fatal to her new-found self.

'I had lunch with my father yesterday and he said he knew of a St Honoré on the island. I thought it was likely that it was the same man.' Leo wandered off and, not wanting to miss a word he said, she began to make up her face instead of defying him and switching on the dryer again. 'Do you know what you're getting into?' he asked quietly. 'Do you know what kind of person he is?'

Her huge, gold-brown eyes met his in the mirror. 'You tell me,' she said, disguising her apprehension with a shrug. She'd met Pascal St Honoré. He was obviously trying to stop her from meeting his father. She was determined to find out why.

Leo scowled and strode over to her, twisting her around on the low stool and holding her wrists firmly. They both stared at her thighs where the robe had fallen away to reveal the fair triangle of soft, downy hair. Leo's jaw quivered and then he roughly covered her again. But they were both shaking.

She saw the lick of his tongue over his lips and quickly moistened hers. Saw his quickened breath lifting his chest in rapid movements. 'Get away from me!' she croaked.

His thick lashes lifted slowly and he looked steadily into her horrified eyes, smiling an infuriatingly mocking smile because she'd revealed her secret desire in that panic-driven sentence.

'First you listen. I've come to warn you, for old times' sake,' he said softly, his mouth and eyes enchanting her, weaving their old spell. Desperately she tried to comprehend what he was saying. 'Vincente St Honoré is not someone you want to be involved with—'

'Vincente?' She furrowed her brow. The father, presumably. Intrigued, she angled her head.

'That's right,' said Leo curtly. 'Don't have anything to do with him.'

'I don't follow your orders,' she snapped.

'You never did,' he grunted. 'But this time, if you don't pay attention to what I'm saying, it could be your funeral.'

Ginny's eyes rounded. 'Why?' she asked shakily. 'Leo, you're scaring me!'

His slate eyes brooded on her for a moment. 'I hope so,' he said soberly, and she knew that he wasn't trying to be malicious, that this was something worryingly serious. Her lower lip began to tremble.

'You'd better explain,' she said apprehensively.

Leo appeared to be considering how much he could tell her. 'I want you to promise that this will go no further,' he said eventually. She nodded, alarm in her huge eyes. 'Many years ago, Vincente St Honoré was part of the international social circuit,' he explained gravely. 'There was a scandal which caused him to be ostracised. Father knows the woman involved in the scandal—someone who was virtually driven insane by the brute.' Leo's mouth curled in scorn. 'She was treated despicably—insulted, humiliated—'

'No,' she whispered, appalled. This was the man who might be her *father*? 'No, Leo!' she cried, not wanting to believe such things.

'So tell me why you've come here to see him,' Leo said tightly.

She wrenched herself free in distress and got up, pacing up and down, thinking of Pascal, and trying to comprehend Leo's story. It all sounded horribly true. If Vincente *was* her father, what would she do? Had he been the reason why her mother had run away and why she had been so disturbed? It was a background she didn't want for herself, blood she didn't relish flowing in her veins.

An unbalanced mother, a brutal father. She went chalk-white with misery, all hope of a happy reunion slowly being extinguished.

'You want a drink?' he asked sharply.

'Yes,' she whispered, waving to the fridge.

In silence she sat while he found the champagne and filled two glasses, coming to stand in front of her. 'You still haven't told me what you're doing flying out to meet this man,' he said. Something in his tone alerted her. He knew more than he was saying and that made her wary.

'My business,' she said shortly.

'Unwise business,' he said, scowling at the champagne in the elegant flute. He reached out and tipped up her chin so that she was forced to look at him. 'Forget any idea of seeing him. There can't be any reason worth the risk. Get dressed. I'll escort you home,' he said gruffly. 'We'll fly back—'

'No! I'm not going!' she cried with defiance.

'You fool!' he scorned. 'What are you expecting from the old lecher?'

Ginny crushed her wince of horror, gave an elegant lift of her shoulders and slid away from him. 'Leave me to run my own life,' she said with cool hauteur. 'I might have a chat with him, I might not. You've told me what you know and it's for me to decide what to do.'

His eyes narrowed menacingly. Hastily she grabbed the dryer and coldly proceeded to dry her hair, ignoring Leo completely. Turmoil raged through her head. Fury too, because nothing was going as she'd planned. She'd imagined a pleasant chat with a middle-aged man who might be her father. And if he wasn't, then at least she would have had a rest on a beautiful island and some sanity in her life at last.

Instead, she was having to believe that Vincente was some terrible old man. She frowned and, despite her worry, suddenly became aware of a change in the atmosphere. Her spine tingled.

Out of the corner of her eye she could see Leo standing with his legs straddled, toffee-dark brows lowered in a thick, temper-driven line and the storm-dark eyes glittering with the intensity of shimmering steel, burning into her neck, while her body acknowledged the feverish chemistry between them by sending flurries of heat across her skin.

It was a sexy, man-will-conquer-woman pose and she was both scared and enthralled by this new ruthlessness of his. Conscious of her nakedness beneath the robe, she slid her long, exposed legs under the dressing table and hurried to finish drying her hair.

Her loins contracted at the very thought of him. Brutally she lifted the brush through her hair, glowering at herself. She couldn't spend eight or nine hours on a plane with him. The more she was near Leo, the more it hurt. The more she wanted him.

'Gorgeous. How long has it been cut?' he murmured idly in her ear, suddenly back-shiveringly close. His fingers lifted strands of the silky hair delicately and she gritted her teeth to stop herself from dropping the dryer.

She turned it up to 'high' so that it was louder. 'A few days!' she yelled. You couldn't be sexy if you were shouting. Leo seemed to think otherwise.

'Very sexy,' he purred, his head bending briefly while he inhaled the scent of her hair. 'It's dry,' he drawled, and she thought for a breathless moment that he was going to nibble her small ear. To her disappointment and relief, he didn't. Firmly he unpicked her fingers from the dryer again and hooked it on the wall then rested his hands on her shoulders and smiled thoughtfully at her reflection in the mirror. She felt a shaft of desire brutalising her body with its searing, cutting edge. 'Why cut it?' he asked softly. 'You always resisted before.'

'I'm here incognito,' she answered sullenly, leaning forward to continue applying her make-up with a rather shaky hand. 'I want privacy and peace. That's one of the reasons I'm here. So you can go home and leave me alone. I don't know why you bothered to come. Why should you care if I get mixed up with this man?'

'Because it will reflect on my family,' he said softly, idly stroking the soft towelling robe. She shouldn't have felt anything, but her back stiffened and contracted beneath his touch.

'It *what*?' she exploded, as much as a release for some of her pent-up feelings as in anger.

Leo's mouth thinned. 'St Honoré is notorious throughout the West Indies. I understand that his son is as bad, taking on his father's mistresses when they're discarded.'

She groaned. It got worse and worse. 'Do you mean Pascal?'

He nodded. 'So get this absolutely clear: I don't know what you think you're doing with the St Honorés, but I won't have you associating with either of them, Virginia!'

'Stop ordering me around!' she snapped. 'I'm not your wife now!'

'No,' he growled. 'But the connection is still there and I refuse to stand by while you bring our name into disrepute—'

'Oh, the Brandon name!' she snapped, sighing extravagantly and adding a yawn for good measure. She picked up a mascara wand and carefully applied the first coat. 'I can't believe what you're saying! Because I was once foolish enough to be married to you, you're asking me to stay away from anyone who might tarnish the reputation of your ridiculously fussy family?' she scathed. Her perfectly shaped eyebrows lifted in astonishment. 'Please! Leave me to manage my life—'

'OK. Have it your own way.' Leo shrugged his big shoulders and started walking away, taking her tension with him. 'The headlines in the papers are full of your disappearance from the jetting scene,' he said, as if it were an afterthought. 'Some talk of kidnap. I'll put them right, of course—tell them where you are and—'

'No! You louse; you wouldn't!' she gasped, leaping to her feet in shock.

'Watch,' he said succinctly. Smugly.

Furious, Ginny flew across to him, grabbing his arm as he reached the top of the steps that led to the external door. 'No, Leo!' she cried urgently. 'I've longed for this time to myself! I'm enjoying being alone! You can't tell the Press!' she half sobbed in angry frustration. 'You don't know how much I need solitude! I want to mingle with ordinary people, to swim and shop, to sunbathe and laze around... Oh, Leo, it's been *years* since I did things like that! And I want to plan the rest of my life—'

'Do you?' His eyes were veiled, his expression unreadable. But he was hesitating.

Ginny's eyes lingered on his mouth. So close. A sudden urge to kiss him overwhelmed her and her lips parted, glistening moistly with desire. 'Be nice; do as I ask for old times' sake,' she coaxed, her voice husky with restrained emotions.

His mouth granted another, unspoken request as he read her like a book. Gently his lips moved over hers, tasting, nibbling, savouring her. He inhaled and she knew that he was breathing in her scented skin as she was inhaling his. Then he was pushing her back a little, his eyes darkly mocking.

'Still a witch, using your charms as a weapon,' he drawled. 'Cheap trick, Ginny. Delightful, though.' She wriggled away, her eyes dark with anger. He smiled secretively. 'Shall we come to an arrangement?' he asked.

Her brows drew together in a suspicious frown and her heart pitter-pattered against her ribs. 'What for?' she asked warily.

Leo smiled again with a smug satisfaction and traced a line from her chin down to the hollow of her throat, sending her brain into reverse in the process. And her body into full steam ahead. She blinked, trying to clear the wool from where wisdom should have been and stop herself submitting to his seduction.

'Let's see,' he murmured, pretending to consider. 'How about this...? I don't reveal who you are to anyone, you steer clear of St Honoré. Then you can have all the solitude and peace you want.'

'Oh.' Her face fell in dismay.

'Not a problem, is it?' he murmured, his finger seemingly fascinated by her collar-bone.

She cleared her throat of the choking lump in it. 'Yes. Leo... I can't steer clear of him.'

'Why?' he asked, a sliver of steel in his eyes.

'There's...there's a very special reason I've come to see him.'

'Which is?' he drawled laconically.

Her huge eyes lifted to his. It would be nice if he understood, she thought. Sharing her hopes and her anxieties with him might help. 'There's a strong possibility he's my father,' she said in a sudden rush.

The trailing finger stilled. She told him then everything she knew. Leo didn't move, but his jaw tightened and his mouth grew harder and grimmer with every second. When she'd finished, she waited, her glistening eyes fixed unblinkingly on his. Which were hostile and frightening.

'I think you're mistaken,' he said stiffly.

'Maybe. But I've got to meet him to find out,' she said with a stubborn set to her mouth. 'He advertised. I read the advert and it mentioned several things about me that virtually no one else could know. I can't just leave this in mid-air. You must understand that. I—I want to find my father very badly. And I must be sure I'm not this man's daughter. There would always be the possibility, Leo. It would be stupid to come so far and not make sure!'

'What if I assure you he couldn't be?'

She blinked in surprise. 'I doubt you could,' she said, puzzled. 'However, if I am convinced he isn't, I'm going to Scotland when I get back. I haven't seen the McKenzies for years and don't really want to, but I have to visit them and question them about my mother and ask them to tell me where I might find her.'

'What for? You haven't bothered till now,' he said with a frown.

'It's not that I couldn't be bothered,' she corrected him quickly. 'I know how she felt about me. I was a nuisance.' Her eyes became pained. 'All I remember is being scrubbed till it hurt. Treated roughly. The smell of disinfectant, and sitting in an uncomfortable, starched dress and not daring to move because the noise made my mother scream. I remember feeling lonely and un-loved. Frightened. Hungry. That's why I didn't want to find her. Now I know I've got to face the past if I'm to make a future.'

'Ginny—'

'No, don't try to dissuade me. I know it won't be easy—any of it—but it's something I have to do, Leo. Until I know about my background, I won't feel I'm a whole person. There are things about me I don't under-stand.' She blushed. Like her deep sexuality. Her head lifted proudly. 'I need to know the whole picture,' she said shakily. 'Good or bad.'

'I see.' There was nothing in his voice to betray his feelings. Not even scorn.

Taking heart, she went on. 'You might find that odd, because my family is unlikely to be anything special. I doubt that I have a long heritage of aristocratic fore-bears like you. Yet my family will have characteristics which will explain me to myself. And I'll learn some-thing by meeting my mother and her relatives. Can you imagine what it's like, not knowing about your background?'

'No. No, I can't,' he acknowledged.

It seemed to Ginny that the more she tried to convince Leo of her purpose, the more she knew that she wouldn't rest till she had found her family. A small and wistful smile wavered on her soft lips.

'Somewhere there are people with my own blood,' she mused huskily. 'People I belong to, who might—' She stopped herself from saying the word 'love'. It hurt even to think it. 'Who might play a part in my life,' she ended feebly.

A huge breath expanded Leo's chest. 'Then if you must speak to St Honoré,' he said softly, 'it's imperative that I am with you, for your own protection.'

Her mouth dropped in dismay. 'No!' she cried sharply.

'I have to stay,' he insisted, his eyes dark and secretive. 'I must make sure St Honoré does nothing to harm you. For the Brandons' sake. You must agree.' His mouth quirked in a sensual, sinister triumph. 'Or,' he added throatily, 'I'll carry out my threat to bring the world's press to your doorstep.'

Ginny's eyes hardened at his threat. But something was liquid inside her at the thought of Leo being near her again, protecting her—even though it was to save his awful family's precious name. Somehow she managed to shape her mouth into a grimace and she glided away from him in case she said, Yes, yes! and ruined everything.

She knew what she wanted and why her heart soared at the thought of spending time with Leo. She wanted her husband back. But that was impossible. Leo and she could never be an item again. He'd made that clear. Although Arabella had married that American film star and was off the scene, there might even be someone else special in his life already—she'd seen several shots of him in social columns in newspapers, squiring gorgeous women. With the usual coy headlines: WILL THEY WED?

To conceal her quiver of horror at the thought, she flung open the doors of the locally carved cedar wardrobe and put her mind to selecting something to wear for her planned trip to Castries, the capital of St Lucia, where she intended to do a little detective work in the library there.

A cotton Klein in all shades of green would do. Soft, understated and cut like a dream to dip in a huge scoop at the neck and cling alluringly where it touched till it reached her hips and flared into gentle swirls.

'Well, Ginny?' Leo murmured menacingly.

'I'd much rather you kept away from me,' she lied with a fair show of distaste. She laid the dress on the bed, wondering why she was so reluctant to save herself from Leo's clutches. 'I'll call Chas to look after me. He's trained to the job.' The smile of triumph she gave him at such a sensible solution was hard and forced.

'Isn't his wife about to give birth?' asked Leo mildly.

Her eyes flickered with irritation. The wretched man knew everything! 'Oh. Yes,' she said, as if she'd forgotten. But a smile lifted the corners of her mouth. She was to be godmother. The smile became wistful. It would be lovely to have a child of her own. A *child*, not an heir. 'That's one of the reasons I didn't ask him to come with me.'

'And the other?'

'Isn't that obvious?' she scathed. 'He'd stand out a mile in these surroundings and everyone would know he's some kind of bodyguard. Fond as I am of him, he does resemble Arnold Schwarzenegger.' She went to search for a pair of comfortable shoes. Green slingback mules. 'I'll dial an escort service in the States,' she muttered, yanking open a drawer and extracting her underwear.

'You'd be recognised in an instant by whoever you chose,' pointed out Leo irritatingly. 'Escorts must read all the gossip pages. You feature on them enough for your escort to make a few thousand dollars by revealing your whereabouts.' When she scowled, an infuriating little smile played about his mouth. 'You know I'm the only man who can fit in this kind of location and look vaguely like your husband—'

'You're *not* my husband,' she said, her voice rising in agitation.

'I'm the only man with the right experience, though,' he drawled. 'I could play the part very well,' he added meaningfully.

Her eyes collided with his—tawny anger and resentment, glittering grey. 'You're not sharing my villa or my bed!' she spat.

'I'd look a funny kind of husband if I didn't,' he pointed out calmly.

Ginny wanted to pull the drawer from the dressing table and throw it at him. To sweep the jars and bottles off the top in a frustrated, helpless temper. But, marshalling all her self-control, she closed the drawer, taking her underwear to the bed. She knew that his eyes were on the flimsy scraps of silk, knew that he was breathing more heavily. And she felt so drained by everything that had happened over the past few years that she wondered if she had enough reserves of emotional energy to stay in charge of the situation.

Logically it was simple. All she had to do was to pretend to Leo that he meant absolutely nothing to her. His masculine pride, that hateful arrogance would be his downfall. He imagined that the minute they were thrown together she'd fall into his arms, that he'd be able to defend his family's honour and satisfy his sex drive at the same time. A double whammy.

Well, he was wrong. Once she'd been burnt. Now she meant to stay away from the fire. The blisters hadn't healed and if she got close again they'd hurt her more than before. Though she had to admit that her resolve became shaky whenever he came close, whenever he turned those smouldering smoke-grey eyes on her and spoke to her in his seductive voice. All he had to do was to say he loved her and she'd fall into his arms. If he ever knew that, she'd be leaping into the flames without a second thought.

Proudly she faced him. Cold, aloof, uninterested. Inwardly she was shaking like a leaf. If he stayed, she'd have to be constantly on her guard. The holiday she'd planned would be ruined till he'd gone and she could behave normally again. They'd be together till she found Vincente St Honoré. Could she face that?

The air between them crackled with an electric charge as she met the full force of his grey, velvety eyes. Her legs were weakening and she sat down quickly on the bed before he noticed. She didn't know what to do. All she could feel was a thrill mounting in intensity as she teetered on the edge of danger.

CHAPTER FOUR

GINNY took a deep breath. She had to jump into the fire one way or the other. If she made every effort to find Vincente, she'd be rid of Leo quickly and then she'd be out of danger.

Something deliciously wicked lurched in her stomach at the thought of spending time with Leo. Still lovesick! She'd got it bad, she mused ruefully.

'The whole idea of your staying here fills me with horror,' she said with icy disdain—and perhaps a smattering of truth. For this new, contemptuous Leo to see her grovel, to see deep inside her and realise that she was obsessed by him would be humiliating in the extreme.

She lifted a pale, proud face to his. 'But since you're obviously set on defending your family honour—and willing to resort to malicious methods to do so—I have to agree. You don't leave me much choice. But I don't like your blackmail and I don't like your reasons. It'll be unpleasant having you around. I'd been looking forward to a relaxing time here.' She tossed her head and a swirl of white-blonde hair shone like shot silk in the sunlight streaming into the room. 'You'll ruin my stay!' she said resentfully. 'And, while we're about it, let's establish some ground rules for your behaviour.'

'Such as?' he murmured smoothly.

'Such as don't get any ideas about intimacy!' she said grimly. 'No sex! Understand?'

'Intimacy? With you?' He wrinkled his aristocratic nose. 'My dear Ginny, I daren't risk it. I don't know where you've been.'

As she dropped her jaw in amazement, he gave her a mocking smile.

'I know who you've been with, though. The papers have carried rather a lot of photographs of you with different escorts,' he purred, but there was an undercurrent of anger in his voice. 'Rakes and roués to a man. Don't insult my intelligence by pretending you haven't partied the last two years away—and don't insult your own beauty by pretending those men went out with you in order to chat about the state of the economy.'

The shutters came down over her eyes. Those parties had filled her time and the emptiness left by knowing that Leo had gone. They'd given her a false sense of fun. One thing she hadn't been able to cope with had been the silence of her own company. Whenever she'd been alone she'd had to face her unhappiness. Partying and dating had kept her from confronting that demon too often and had helped to stop her from cracking up.

The men she'd dated she had done so on the understanding that they took her home and left her unmolested. They hadn't refused because they'd been keen to have the publicity. She smiled wryly.

'I've partied a little,' she said in an offhand manner.

His mouth thinned in disdain. 'A lot!'

Ginny frowned. 'How do you know?'

'Contacts,' he said tersely.

'Spies,' she suggested, her expression frosty.

Leo looked haughty. 'I'm relieved that this is only a temporary arrangement and I can get back to people who have deeper values than you,' he muttered. 'I'd better get my bags moved in. Where's the phone?'

'There isn't one. No TV, radio or piped Muzak. This is solitude, Leo, an inaccessible hideaway.'

'Suits me. No sex, no TV. What *will* you do of an evening?' he asked insultingly.

'I hope most of the time I'll be talking to my father over a Planter's Punch,' she said shortly.

He made a face. 'I can't say I hope your wishes will come true. St Honoré has too vile a reputation to be anyone's father. He isn't yours, that's for sure.'

'How could you possibly know?' she asked, shaken by his conviction.

He frowned at the floor and she felt certain that he had a good reason to be so confident. Her palms sweated and she rubbed them on her robe as she remembered her earlier suspicion that he wasn't telling her everything her knew.

'Intuition,' he said, dissembling. 'It doesn't seem credible that your mother was married to him. Father told me that Vincente's wife was some society woman. She came from Britain, but she wasn't as poor as a church mouse. She...had money in her own right. I know your mother didn't have a penny. You told me. And the McKenzies told *you* that she had nobody to support her. It doesn't tie up with what we know of Vincente's wife. She fled from St Lucia and arrived back in England in some distress.'

'So?' she challenged, puzzled.

'We look after our own, Ginny,' he explained. 'Vicente's wife would have been cared for. Your mother was on her own. For us there's an old-school network, a closing of ranks and a protection of one another. Even if Mrs St Honoré's family disowned her—though I see no reason why they should—someone who'd known her in the social circuit would have taken her in, even as a governess or a companion.'

'I suppose you can't have members of ancient dynasties dying before their time,' she said, feeling waspish about the British aristocracy.

'Don't knock it,' he retorted curtly. 'It's a generous tradition and we're not the only community to practise it. Wouldn't Chas's wife be taken in by family, friends or neighbours if something happened to him?'

'Yes,' she admitted reluctantly, thinking that the same wouldn't be true of the people in her line of business. Everyone lived for money and fame. There was no time for consoling those who'd fallen by the wayside. 'I suppose so—'

'You do hate to admit you're in the wrong!' he said drily. 'Our community might be more scattered than Chas's, but it is intensely loyal. That's why we spend country weekends together. And why we meet regularly on social occasions. It renews our bonds of friendship and keeps them going.'

'I remember,' muttered Ginny. Ascot. Gstaad. Polo at Cowdray Park. Ghastly weekends with nothing to say to anyone because she didn't know anything about fishing or hunting or shooting. Or the million ties that bound Leo's set. Horrible. She'd always felt like an exotic butterfly in a cage.

'I accept that there's an instinct of group-preservation in what we do,' Leo mused. 'I find that laudable. Our families have a long history, Ginny. Only by cleaving together do we protect that history.'

'Often at the expense of love,' she said quietly.

Leo's eyes narrowed. 'It's easier if people from the same social group marry one another,' he said with chilling detachment. 'They know what to expect.'

'I never fitted in,' she agreed levelly. 'Nor did I want to, to be honest. Some of the hallowed traditions are archaic! And you were so determined to be well-mannered that you didn't object when, for instance, we women were hustled out after dinners so you men could indulge in men's talk!'

'I was brought up never to offend my host,' he said quietly. 'Should I have ruined everyone's evening and insisted you stayed?'

'No,' she said hopelessly. 'It's the tradition itself that I can't stomach.'

'Amber understands. She doesn't rail at the way other people live their lives,' he said in reproach.

Ginny thought of Leo's father's red-headed god-daughter and sighed. 'Amber and I are poles apart,' she said wryly. 'She's mad about Castlestowe, for a start. Her idea of heaven is walking on the moors when it's raining. I can't be like her! I know you and she were virtually brought up together and you probably compare her with me constantly, but you shouldn't expect me to fit into your life the way she does! She was born to it. I wasn't.'

'Ginny,' he said softly, 'it's over.' A spasm ran through her body, visible and mortifying. 'So,' he said with a brutal cheerfulness, 'you hate the British upper class but you're hoping to become part of island society! Very contrary, Ginny! Don't you see how unlikely it is that you're Vincente's daughter? I don't know why you don't admit that and forget him.'

Absently, she picked up her undies, sifting the silk through her fingers. His comments had worried her. All she wanted was a house somewhere quiet and private, with Leo, children and good friends. Close friends, not hordes of hangers-on or people she couldn't relate to.

The thought of joining a society family was filling her
with horror.

'I need to be sure,' she sighed. She looked up. 'We'll
find Vincente fast,' she said anxiously, eager to get it
over and done with. And, since she wasn't going to be
playing happy homes with Leo, it would help if he was
off the scene fast too. 'Then we can be shot of each
other,' she added shakily.

'Suits me,' he muttered, and she gritted her teeth to
stop herself wincing at his eagerness to leave.

'Whatever happens here, I'll start searching for my
mother soon,' she said, her face wistful.

'Do you really think that's a good idea? I'd go with
your earlier gut feelings to leave her strictly alone if I
were you,' he said quickly, beetling his thick brows
together.

'No,' she retorted firmly. 'I'm sorting everything out.
I need to know things.'

Leo seemed about to tell her something and then
thought better of it, drawing up a chair and sitting in
front of her. 'I know you're not in the mood to listen
to a lecture so I'll say this,' he began gravely. She made
to move away and he took her hands in his to stay her.
'Please. Pay attention for your mother's sake,' he ordered. His eyes bored into hers, mesmerising her. 'If you
ever do find her, I want you to promise me that you'll
spend more time with her than you did with me.'

Ginny lowered her eyes guiltily. There had always been
reasons for her hectic life. 'I know what you're implying,' she muttered. 'In your eyes I was a bad wife
and I'd have been an even worse daughter. But I had
something to prove to myself—'

'You wanted people to like you,' he said bluntly.

She thought about that. 'I think you're right. It was a novelty,' she admitted slowly, and heaved a heavy sigh. At first the adulation had done wonders for her self-esteem. Lately... Her head lifted. It meant nothing any more. She'd lost what she'd wanted: Leo. 'We all like to be special,' she said in a low voice. 'It was evident that my mother and my adoptive parents didn't like me much—'

'I did. I liked you,' he said quietly, his thumb massaging the pronounced ball of her thumb. 'Wasn't that enough?'

Ginny tried to focus on something other than the effect of his rhythmical caress which was causing such havoc in her body. Deliberately she concentrated on a cooing Zenaida dove picking up crumbs from the deck where she'd had breakfast. The tantalising sensation trickling through her veins mercifully receded a little.

He'd said 'liked'. Not love. And he'd used the past tense.

'You met me when I was already on my way to being really famous,' she said stiffly. 'I never knew what I was to you because of that. I'd worked for years to be regarded as a beautiful woman instead of a gangling beanpole,' she went on, her mouth wry. 'And when I finally made it I didn't know if men wanted me for myself or because I was good to look at and having me on their arm did things for their ego. It was like being at school again, trying to avoid the bullying by handing out sweets and never feeling too sure why the crowd formed around me.'

'You thought you'd found paradise in your job, didn't you?' he murmured, taking her chin in his hand, turning her face towards him and looking deep into her eyes again.

Nothing would stop her body trembling. Mute and miserable, she remained a prisoner of his gaze, a captive of the love she felt for him, drowning in his smouldering eyes and wishing, wishing that they could live together somehow, anyhow. She didn't care.

'Paradise...' she whispered hoarsely. It was in his eyes, his hands, the tender smile on his mouth. Paradise was Leo. And once she'd thought it was somewhere else—in a league table of achievement, in being the most photographed model of the year.

His fingers caressed her soft skin. His lashes fluttered on his cheeks and when he looked up again his eyes were unreadable. 'And you found that even paradise wasn't perfect,' he husked. 'So you kept on trying to make it perfect by trying harder.' He smiled cynically. 'There is no paradise, Ginny. Very beautiful women, handsome men, the very rich still have problems.'

'Different problems,' she breathed.

'Sure.' He no longer touched her, holding her still by the mesmeric power of his eyes alone. 'But none the less frustrating. Some folk spend a lifetime striving for the perfect life but when—if—they get it they discover they want something else after all. And that they've sacrificed something they'd give their eye-teeth to possess again.' His voice dropped to a mutter and he seemed to be struggling for words. 'But, of course, it's unobtainable,' he said quietly. 'They've gone too far to go back for it and it's lost for ever.'

He seemed sad, as if his life wasn't perfect, and she wondered what else he could possibly want. He had it all. Money, family, any woman he wanted. 'What would be your paradise?' she asked in a rasp. Her emotions were in a knot. She'd lost more than she'd ever dreamed possible.

The rain-grey eyes seemed to shimmer with an inner light. 'There's only one thing that I think is worthwhile. One dream that I have. To be married to the woman who is mother to my child,' he said huskily.

Ginny flinched as if from a blow. Before she spoke she had to clear her throat of the obstruction there. 'You'll find her,' she said bleakly.

Leo firmed his mouth. 'Actually, Ginny, I've already met the woman I want to live with for the rest of my life,' he replied softly.

And Ginny could barely keep her face rigid. Frantically she struggled to mask her feelings. Something was paralysing her, otherwise she'd have stood, walked away, hidden her expression. But she had to stick it out and look back at him as if she didn't give a damn.

Whereas in reality her heart was breaking. The nightmare scenario that had haunted her for so long had finally come true. Her beloved Leo had found the true love of his life. And the tragedy was that it wasn't *her*.

The loneliness overwhelmed her. There were only two other people who might possibly care for her with any depth—and both were elusive, shadowy figures. Both might disappoint her and shatter her faith in human nature. But the hope of finding her parents was all she had to cling to now.

'I want to find my father. I want my mother, Leo!' she said miserably. Try as she might to stop them, the tears began to fall in torrents. 'Oh, Leo!' she mumbled, holding out her arms to him in a hopeless, helpless movement.

After hesitating, his face devoid of all expression, he gave a sigh and drew her onto his lap. Warm, comforting, secure. And she buried her face in his warm, male-scented neck, unsure whether she was crying for her missing mother or herself. Both, probably. Her sorrow swung with a butterfly restlessness from her own misery to the terrible life that her mother must have known.

'Sorry to break down like that...' she began apologetically.

'Understandable,' he growled, but she could tell that he was irritated by her need for him. He held her awkwardly, as though he didn't want her too close but was comforting her as a kindness for old times' sake.

'I keep thinking of my poor mother, Leo!' she husked, hoping he wouldn't think that she was crying because she felt abandoned by him. 'I was thinking what it must have been like for her to be alone with a baby she didn't want and so miserable that she let strangers take me away! Can you imagine how hard life must have been for her? I want to hold her and say it's all right, Leo. I want to tell her that I understand—' Her face crumpled. 'I want the answers to my questions now,' she mumbled.

Leo's mouth breathed warmth on her cheekbones as he murmured words of sympathetic agreement and simultaneously calmed her with small patting movements of his hands, as a rider might do with a high-spirited, temperamental filly. It should have been insulting but it was nice—too nice. Alarmed, she slid off his lap.

'I need to dress,' she said harshly. 'Go and see the people in Reception and get your things transferred here.'

'Relax,' he murmured. 'You obviously need someone to comfort you—'

'No!' she yelled, moving back as he stepped forward. She forgot that the bed was behind her and fell backwards onto it. 'I don't want your pity! Go away!' she screamed, scrambling awkwardly across the bed and to the other side.

Leo didn't move a muscle but there was a faintly self-satisfied smile lifting the corners of his mouth that infuriated her.

'I don't want you to hold me; I don't want your vile hands anywhere near me. You stay here as long as it takes for me to find out if this Vincente is on the level or not and then you go. Understand?' she spat.

Leo smiled more broadly. The cat looked as if it had the cream in that smile. 'I understand very well. And soon you will too.'

'I understand *now*! This arrangement is for our convenience,' she said, grabbing all the frayed edges of her temper and cobbling together a temporary mend. 'I need something, you need something and unfortunately we have to be together to achieve that. Maybe neither of us wants to be thrown together. Certainly I'd rather pretend to be married to Godzilla if he was around! But I don't know anyone I can trust so we're stuck with each other—'

'For better, for worse,' he put in helpfully.

Ginny glared. 'This is going to be a nightmare!' she muttered. 'Go and get your stuff moved here since you have to, but stay in the bar and have a few coffees. I want to do my workout before I start making enquiries about Vincente St Honoré. There's no point in you being around while I exercise.'

'You're on one of the most beautiful islands in the West Indies and you want to do a workout in your room?' asked Leo incredulously.

'Well, I'm not doing it in public!' she snapped, bristling. 'I have to take care of my body—'

'Sure,' he soothed. 'And the results are spectacular. So you're going to put on your leotard,' he mused. 'Are you hoping to seduce me?'

Ginny spluttered with fury. 'No!' she snapped. 'Darn it! You're arrogant! I'm not interested, Leo!'

'I see,' he said, injecting a wealth of doubt into those two simple words. 'I wasn't sure why you hadn't rushed to put some clothes on before now,' he explained. 'I thought you were hoping I might make a pass.'

'Wrong,' she said tightly and without being certain that she was telling the truth. Her inner needs seemed to be warring with her desire to protect her emotions.

'Funny. I could have sworn... I must be wrong,' he said blandly. 'I thought you sort of melted when you sat on my lap.'

'Muscle fatigue. I'm tired,' she said grimly.

'Then you ought to take a break. You're looking terrible,' he observed casually, smiling when she blinked in surprise and cautiously touched her face. 'No, nothing's dropped off,' he said in amusement. 'But you're bad-tempered, skinnier than before, there are bags under your eyes and your skin isn't *quite* as blooming as it used to be. Your lifestyle's telling on you.'

Of course it was! How could she glow and bloom without Leo? The lack of sleep and constant depression had taken all the sparkle from her eyes and the freshness from her complexion. And it hurt her that Leo should have noticed the difference and had found her less than perfect.

'I'm taking a break, aren't I?' she said resentfully.

'Exercises, snatched meals, no doubt, rushing around like a demented chicken...' His mouth twitched at her indignant glare. 'Slow down,' he murmured. 'Stop fitting things into your schedule.' His innocent smile lit his face. 'You're in a beautiful place; why not enjoy it and spend the day on the beach?'

'I have things to do,' she said suspiciously. 'Are you suggesting I shouldn't ever work hard at getting what I want?'

'No. You had to in the past for all sorts of reasons,' he conceded. 'I know only too well that you have to dedicate yourself wholeheartedly if you want to achieve an important goal. However, I am suggesting you stop now and enjoy yourself. Squander your time. Be indulgent. It's a wonderful world out there. I bet you haven't stretched out in the sun here and done nothing at all for a whole day. Mind you, I doubt you could,' he mused. 'Too frenetic. Too hyper—'

'As a matter of fact,' she said haughtily, revising her plans on the spot just to confound him, 'you're wrong. I *have* been lounging around for the past few days. And I'm going to the beach after I've chatted to the people in Reception about Vincente.'

'Oh.' He glanced at the dress which she'd laid out on the bed. It wasn't suitable for the beach but he didn't question her choice. 'My mistake. You do know how to relax.' His eyes twinkled at her. 'I'm wrong. Apologies.'

Leo sauntered out, whistling softly to himself. Hastily she rummaged in a drawer for her leotard and began her routine. Halfway through, one elegant long leg suspended in mid-air, she began to wonder whether Leo had actually manipulated her into wasting time when she'd really wanted to hunt down Vincente.

It had been Leo who'd suggested the day on the beach. Where would that get him? Did he think he could help her with her sunblock and torment her by talking about the precious summer days they'd spent together when it had been his delight—and hers—to massage oil into her skin? Slowly a broad smile crept across her face as she remembered how that had usually ended up.

'I didn't know exercises could be so amusing!' marvelled Leo in mock surprise.

Ginny flung him a flustered glance and began to scissor her incomparable legs at a furious rate. 'You were supposed to stay drinking coffee,' she said coldly.

'I did. Two cups. And I chatted to someone called Agnes. She knows the St Honoré family. Hey, no, don't interrupt your routine,' he said in consternation when she made to get up. 'You keep going and I'll tell you what I learned.'

Ginny quivered at the interest in his eyes as he assessed her curves in the skimpy leotard. What could she do now? Further scissor movements were out of the question—too pneumatic. She didn't want to do anything that might appear seductive. Something innocuous. Hamstring stretch? She felt the power of his eyes burning into her and felt prickles of heat curling into her pelvis.

One of them—or both?—seemed to be breathing more heavily. Performing in front of a suspicious and critical Leo was terrible. Her routine had always turned him on. He'd be making comparisons with those days when he'd watched her with hunger and yearning in his eyes.

Now he sprawled on her tumbled bed and showed only amused detachment. Grimly Ginny persevered, carrying out the routine rather badly and feeling angry and unsatisfied with herself as a result. Somehow her body wouldn't respond. It was tight and tense—and yet weak at the same time.

Neck-rolls were about the only thing that wouldn't be interpreted as a turn-on, she thought gloomily. And she discovered after a moment that even they meant a lot of hair-tossing. She flung her head back, hot and bothered, and met his drowsy-lidded eyes, their ex-

pression unreadable. Her breath quickened. Was he remembering the same thing? That moment when she'd
cast aside all inhibitions and their bodies had melted
together in a hot frenzy?

Damn him! she thought angrily. Damn, damn, damn
him!

'My, you're breathing heavily,' he commented. There
was a maddeningly suggestive smile on his lips.

'I did some extremely vigorous exercises a few moments before you came back,' she lied, trying to keep
the irritated edge out of her voice. 'You said you'd tell
me about St Honoré. So give.'

'Hmm? Oh, yes. Sorry,' he said with an insincere
smile, his gaze glued to the curve of her buttocks.

It was too much. Her breathing was almost impossible to keep under control. Ginny ran through a rapid
cool-down and stopped. 'I've finished,' she said abruptly.

'You have a new short routine?' he enquired with
interest, his mouth quirking at her quick glare. 'Hardly
worth changing for.' Languidly he stretched the whole
length of his powerful body then shifted to the edge of
the bed. 'And I'm wasting good sunshine, hanging
around in here watching you lurching around like an
asthmatic automaton.' Ginny's eyes glittered with ice-
green lights and he grinned disarmingly. 'I think I'll grab
my things from my case and go down to the beach.'

'But... what about Vincente?' she protested.

'My news will wait. I can talk in the sun as well as
indoors,' he said drily. 'Come and find me— Oh, and
don't forget we're married, will you?'

'I'll sharpen my tongue especially,' she snapped.

Leo laughed and wagged his finger at her. 'No. It won't
be that kind of marriage, Ginny. We'll be madly in love.
If word is to get back to Vincente that I'm your pro-

tector, he must know I'm attentive and jealous. You do understand that, don't you?' he said calmly.

'You worm!' she muttered in disgust. 'You only want a chance to make me cringe by putting your hands all over me—'

'Not in the least. Wherever did you get that idea? In fact I'd prefer not to touch you unless the occasion calls for it,' he drawled, and she flushed, cut down to size. 'To be honest, I'd rather not be seduced by you, so save your efforts for someone who'd appreciate them.

'It's a matter of keeping myself for better things, you know,' he explained suavely. 'Fortunately, I think I've become immune to your attractions. That's why I was watching you with such interest just now. I find it fascinating to note that before I would have become wildly aroused by the movement of your supple body. Suddenly it holds no mysteries, no thrills for me any more. How times change.'

Open-mouthed, Ginny watched him saunter over to his luggage. Angry and shaking from the blow of his insult, she stalked to the shower, banged the door shut and sluiced herself down. When she emerged, he'd gone—and it was just as well. Her fingers still itched to slap his smug, malicious face.

Running to lock the front door, she raced back up the stairs and dropped her robe to check herself in the mirror. No flaws that she could see. Tall, slender, with generous breasts for her weight. Tiny waist, curvy hips and rear. Skin... She peered closely with a critical eye. Smooth as honey.

But... Her brow seemed to have faint lines on it. There *were* bags under her eyes. Hastily, afraid that she'd lose her only asset—her looks—she smoothed on some moisturiser and grinned wryly at herself when she checked the mirror again to see if it had made any difference.

'Lord, you're paranoid!' she said ruefully. 'You *do* need a spot of normality!'

A few more days of rest would do the trick. Preferably without Leo criticising her appearance. She winced, yearning for the days when he'd told her that she was always beautiful to him—and would be so even when she was old and grey. That had made her very happy. But now he was probably comparing her with the woman he wanted to marry.

She drew in a long, shuddering breath. Leo would have children by that woman. Her reflection blurred as misery flooded through her body. Leo was hers. *Hers!* And yet she had to get used to the idea that he was on the brink of committing himself body and soul to another woman.

Her shaking hands covered her face and she wondered why she couldn't seem to get it into her thick head that her relationship with Leo was over.

If only he hadn't turned up! She must meet Vincente as soon as possible. Then she could wave Leo goodbye. A tremor of regret flickered for a brief moment in her mind before she ruthlessly suppressed it. He was bad for her. He didn't like her any more—and actively despised her. So she might as well accept that and get a life elsewhere.

Years of experience in blocking out her emotions and willing herself to follow a particular path came into play again. Leo had been a mistake she'd regret for ever. But she knew better than most how to focus her mind on a particular goal—and this time that goal was her self-respect and inner peace.

Leo made her feel cheap and unworthy. He aroused her emotions. Far better to cut him from her heart than to suffer his wounds over and over again.

Ginny slipped a turquoise T-shirt and shorts over her fuchsia-coloured bathing costume and went to look for Agnes, hoping to bypass the chat with Leo.

'Agnes has gone off duty,' said a helpful bar-boy.

She peered at his name badge. Simon. 'I'm looking for Vincente St Honoré, Simon,' she said in a friendly tone. 'Do you know him? Or is there anyone here who might tell me about him and where I can find him?'

The young man lowered his huge dark eyes and shifted his bare feet around on the tiled terrace of the deserted restaurant. 'He disappeared. People here don't know where he is.'

'Agnes knows,' she persisted, certain that Simon was avoiding a straight answer.

'Agnes has gone home,' repeated Simon sullenly.

'OK. Thanks,' she said with a cool smile. It would have to be Leo, then. 'Which way to the beach?' she asked pleasantly.

'Down there, lady.' Simon pointed to a flight of steps, sounding relieved.

She thanked him again and followed the twisting steps of volcanic rock that ran in a zigzag fashion down the hill, catching occasional glimpses of a golden beach and a glittering blue sea between the dense greenery of tropical vegetation. It looked very inviting and she felt her tension easing with every step.

Her only worry was that she might be recognised, but since the hotel only housed a small number of people the beach wasn't crowded and hardly anyone glanced her way as she wandered across the hot sand, searching for Leo.

Even if they did realise who she was, she had the feeling that people would be far too polite to rush up and plague her anyway. It was a nice feeling to be a private person again.

Leo was lying out in the sun beside a thatched beach shelter. His eyes were closed and he looked completely at ease. Several paperbacks were piled on the shelf beneath the shelter and Ginny felt their lure immediately. As a teenager she'd read avidly while waiting for photographers and agents at 'go-sees'—the auditions for aspiring models. And she'd enjoyed diving into books during the last few days she'd spent at the hotel. It had been ages since she'd had time to enjoy anything more than brief magazine articles.

Carefully sitting herself in the shade a foot away from Leo, she leaned back in the comfortable lounger and stretched out with a soft sigh of pleasure. 'Tell me about Vincente,' she prompted.

'Didn't you ask Agnes on your way down?' he murmured drowsily.

Ginny looked over at him sharply. He knew her too well! 'Agnes is off duty,' she said drily.

His mouth quirked but his eyes remained annoyingly shut. 'So, it'll have to be me!'

'Yes.' She waited for a while then saw that he was going to make her crawl. 'Get on with it!' she muttered. 'Vincente. Tell me what you know.'

'Got a problem there,' he drawled.

She sat up. 'Why?' she asked suspiciously.

'Looks like you might have to wait a while before he can see you. Agnes says he's in hospital.'

Her face fell in disappointment. 'Oh. That explains why he hasn't come to see me.'

'She said she thought he'd be out soon. We'd better wait till he contacts you, I suppose. I expect word will get back to him that you've been enquiring,' he said idly. 'It usually does in places like this. Incidentally, I made sure Agnes knew that I was your husband and deeply suspicious of anyone and everything. Vincente will think twice before doing anything untoward to you.' He lifted one eyelid, squinted at her and smiled. 'Thought you were going to wear that green dress affair?' he murmured.

'That was... I got that out ready in case Vincente could see me immediately,' she said defensively. No way was she going to admit that Leo had persuaded her to change her mind about taking a taxi to Castries and to lounge on the beach instead!

He chuckled as if he'd already worked that fact out and Ginny scowled. But Leo's eyes were closed again, his face bathed in sunshine. His body was still well honed. How, she didn't know. He played squash and tennis, rode, and was ever active on the estate, but he didn't spend hours in the gym. Her gaze dawdled over the achingly familiar contours and when she met his eyes again she started, because they were fixed steadily on her.

'Don't be so defensive,' he murmured lazily. 'I'm not going to leap on you, remember? Grab a paperback, read, sleep, do nothing, Ginny. You might discover that you like it.' And he closed his eyes, settling down firmly for a long bask in the sun.

By the end of the day she'd added to her earlier joy of slowing her life down to a crawl after running ragged for too many years. The novel was entertaining and amusing, lying down in the warm air was wonderful, and swimming in the deep blue Caribbean was out of this world.

She got even better at relaxing after three further days of complete idleness. Leo didn't make any overtures to her at night, and merely bade her a polite goodnight, wandering off to his bedroom as though they were old friends instead of ex-lovers. Sometimes he'd put his arm around her shoulder or her waist in public, and he always acted like an affectionate husband whenever they chatted to fellow guests. But he never once stepped out of line.

And the trouble was that she wished he would. Sometimes when she lay in bed, wide awake and restless, she thought that it would be nice to have a reason to slap him down, tell him that he was wasting his time. Sometimes she was more honest and admitted to herself that if she had the choice—without any strings attached—she'd climb into his bed and curl up beside him.

She knew that she was behaving like a fool; that she should ice him out and stop enjoying herself so much. They swam, sunbathed and had taken up snorkelling. There was a lot of laughter between them, a lot of casual, no-big-issue talking. For the first time in years she felt carefree and happy.

And it hurt. Because she had to keep up the appearance of being happily married and seemed to be doing a pretty good job of it. Without sex between them and the pressures from outside, it was obvious that they could have been good friends.

'Tennis at eight in the morning?' Leo called, on his way to his room on the third night.

'Lovely,' she replied, and meant it.

'Dinner was fun.' He'd turned and was smiling at her.

She smiled back. They'd been part of a large and friendly group—some local people as well as guests—

and she'd had a ball. 'Hysterical! Was it the daiquiris or were everyone's stories really side-splitting?'

Leo moved back into the darkness of his room. All she could see were his gleaming eyes and the paleness of his blue shirt-front, lit by the flickering candles dotted around the living area. 'Both,' he said huskily. 'And we're less stressed out than we've been for a long time. I'm enjoying this break, Ginny.'

For a moment she hesitated, then said, 'Me too. Goodnight, Leo.' Her voice was wistful. Hastily she turned away and busied herself unnecessarily with plumping up cushions.

'Goodnight. Look forward to our tennis in the morning.'

She could only manage a muttered acknowledgement. His door closed and she sank down on the sofa, staring into space, her emotions choking her. It didn't seem to matter how often she tried to talk sense into her stupid brain, she seemed determined to rush headlong towards her own destruction like a mesmerised lemming.

She was in love with Leo and always would be. And as soon as Vincente no longer posed a threat to his wretched family Leo would desert her and she'd be heading for hell.

CHAPTER FIVE

'YOU'RE staring at me!' she said a little self-consciously the next morning at breakfast. To hide her discomfort, she lifted the napkin from the bread-basket and threw bits of warm croissant to the black grackles, the glossy black birds which spent a happy couple of hours each morning scavenging from soft-hearted guests.

'I was thinking how quickly your glow has come back,' Leo said casually, checking over her face and where her skin had been bared by her crimson halter-neck top.

She beamed, her eyes alight with pleasure. 'Really?' And she covered her delight by saying lightly, 'Thank heavens! I'm fit for the cameras again!'

'That's your fourth croissant,' he observed drily. 'Not eating for two, are you?'

Her heart somersaulted with the pain. Chance would be a fine thing. 'No. Hungry, that's all. Four?' she squawked in horror, recovering her equilibrium fast. 'I'll need two workouts, that game of tennis and a two-hour jog to get rid of them!'

'Such discipline! Bit of a drag, isn't it?' he murmured.

It was. She'd rather spend the time with Leo, lounging around doing nothing. Fortunately she didn't have to answer. One of the guests was approaching them—someone she would normally have been a little wary of because he was something of a flirt. Needing the diversion, she waved her fingers at him in welcome.

'Hello, Lionel! Doing anything exciting today?'

He came up close and put his hand on her bare shoulder, a leer on his slack mouth. 'You're the most exciting thing I'd like to do, Virginia!' he breathed.

Leo's chair crashed back. He was around the table and lifting Lionel off his feet before Ginny could blink. 'I'm a jealous man, Lionel,' he said in a low, menacing whisper. 'And very possessive. I protect my wife from any unpleasantness.'

'Leo! Please!' hissed Ginny, embarrassed.

Slowly he lowered the startled Lionel to the ground but kept his fists wrapped around handfuls of the man's Bagshaw shirt while startled guests and waitresses looked on in fascination. 'I think your remark went a little beyond the pale, don't you?' he suggested quietly. 'More in keeping with bar talk to a whore than breakfast conversation with a lady. I'm sure you'd like to apologise.'

Leo was smiling pleasantly now, but his mouth was thin-lipped and there was a malevolent glitter in his darkened eyes. Ginny drew in her breath. His stance, his taut muscles—even the jerking of the pulse in his hard jaw-line—were all giving the right message: a man offended by an insult to a lady. His lady.

The irony didn't escape her as Lionel apologised and she murmured rather sympathetic words of acknowledgement. Because Leo had been acting out a farce for everyone else's benefit and she was the last person he'd categorise as having an honour worth defending.

After a decent interval she left to sit on the bar terrace while Leo went to change. She'd insisted that she wanted a few moments to herself, because she didn't want to talk about the incident. It had been a strain chatting intimately with him and putting her hand on his in gentle appeasement whenever his smouldering eyes had flicked over to Lionel's table in the far corner.

Leo's chivalrous defence had been like a sword in her side. He'd behaved like that when they were first married, and her self-esteem had soared as a result. For once, she hadn't been a nuisance, clumsy, skinny or ugly. Nor had she been a slightly unreal, manufactured beauty, to be stared at and criticised, tugged this way and that by designers, photographers and the public alike.

She had been a wife. Someone precious and worthy of a man's protection. If only! A spasm distorted her face and she frowned in annoyance at her useless whining. He didn't respect her now and never would. And he'd cheated on her, hadn't he?

That had been something she'd never come to terms with, had never understood. It had seemed so unlike him and his sense of honour.

Leo wandered past in his tennis whites. Her turn to change. Quickly she ran up the hill to the villa. And there, slipping a twisted scarf around her hair to draw it off her face, she reflected ruefully that she'd need a tougher skin if she was to survive the next few days of being 'married' to the supposedly jealous Leo. There would be other moments when his actions would wound her because they were only for show.

Her tawny eyes grew sad. Introducing him to Vincente would be a bad moment. The man was presumably hopeful that he'd found his long-lost daughter. However wicked he was, he must have some good feelings—sentiment, family love—if he'd been prepared to fork out for the plane tickets and accommodation in St Lucia for that hope.

So if he did turn out to be her father she'd then be faced with telling him some time that virtually her first words to him had been a lie and Leo wasn't her husband at all. What would he think of her then? Ginny sighed.

It wasn't a good basis on which to begin building what must inevitably be a difficult relationship.

If only her marriage could be resurrected from the dead!

'Oh-h-h!' she growled in exasperation, grabbing her racket. 'Life gets so complicated!'

In a simple sleeveless tennis shirt and skirt, her face devoid of all make-up, she joined Leo on the tennis courts. Seeing him there, leaning against a jacaranda tree, achingly handsome in the white, white shorts and shirt, she wished that she could go back to their first meeting and start again.

There must be a way. Excitement lit her eyes. There *was* an answer—somewhere! She truly believed that there was an answer to every problem. The trouble came when you wanted to find it!

'You seem eager to start,' Leo murmured silkily when she came to stand by him.

Ginny stopped swishing her racket and jiggling up and down. 'Warming up,' she said succinctly.

'I'll warm you up.'

The words had been husked slowly, quietly, and they'd driven right through any defences she might have had snuggling down in all the empty corners of her body. Tense and expectant, she waited for his pass, ready to deflect it. It never came.

'When you've played the first set,' he promised, his ardent eyes fixed on hers, 'you'll be as warm as you could desire.'

'Huh!' she scorned, sweeping a too real hot desire from those treacherous corners. '*You'll* be the one in a sweat. I've been having professional lessons.'

'Sweetheart,' he said languidly, easing his long frame from the jacaranda and picking up his racket, 'I don't need lessons. I go on instinct and reaction.' He smiled obliquely at her. 'I think you get more depth of stroke that way.' His smile broadened when she slanted him a suspicious look. 'Shall I toss for the game?'

'Heads,' she muttered.

'I win. A good omen. My serve. I do hope you're ready for this.'

Wondering if the smooth tones really did contain the hidden nuances she thought she detected, she looked at him harder. Pure innocence shone on his face. That was so unlikely a condition where he was concerned that she felt wary immediately.

'I'm ready to return anything that comes my way,' she said calmly, and walked to the far end, anything but calm.

He won the set. Her agitation, the powerful confrontation of his male athleticism worked against her skill.

Several times she thought that *she* was winning and had a chance. It seemed not. Weakening her knees with his elation, Leo played subtle shots—underhand, tricky stuff which had her racing up and down the court after maverick balls and just failing to reach them.

They'd gathered quite a crowd and she played harder. So did he, teasing her with better lobs than hers, infuriating her with delicate drop-shots and blasting her occasionally with fiercely driven forehands that came close to knocking the racket out of her hand.

'Game, set, et cetera!' he called, slamming a brutal backhand into the far corner.

A ripple of applause came from the sidelines and several of their new-found friends shouted out congratulations to them both, because she'd put up a fight she could be proud of, faced with such a devastating opponent.

Leo leapt showily over the net, threw down his racket, whipped hers from her hand and laughed exultantly. He picked her up, his hands on her waist, like an adoring lover, and whirled her around till she was dizzy and laughing too. And trembling so much that she thought he'd know that every bone in her body had surrendered game and match to him a long time ago.

Then she felt herself being lowered to the ground and he had taken her hot, sweating face in his.

'Happily married, sweetheart,' he said in warning, when she made to pull back in alarm. 'Arms around my neck, big clinch. Ready?'

'Beast!' she whispered, seduced against her will by his warm chuckle.

And, beaten as she was, a devil entered her mind and told her not to be beaten twice in the same morning. He wanted to play with fire? He'd get an inferno!

So she sighed, 'Darling, you were wonderful!' then smiled alluringly and wrapped her arms obediently around his neck, pulling his head down till his mouth met hers.

A few people cheered and laughed. Ginny concentrated all her heart, all her love in the kiss, murmuring into his mouth, opening his lips with her tongue. Her hand idly rested against his heaving chest. As her kiss intensified, so did the heaving, and so did her hopes.

Her lashes fluttered and she stole a surreptitious glance from beneath them. He was watching her carefully and she froze.

'Don't stop, Delilah,' he murmured sardonically, infuriatingly in control of himself. 'You're making a very good job of being a besotted wife.'

Reluctantly she wriggled away, annoyed that her best effort hadn't been good enough to weaken his brain.

Laughing at her cross face, he lifted her off her feet again. It was a trick he'd often used when she'd argued with him in the past and it always irritated her like mad.

'Put me down!' she demanded sullenly.

'I'm very tempted to drop you among the screwpines, or straight in the sea,' he mused. 'You have a wicked habit of trying to lure me into your clutches.'

'You started it!' she accused, feeling stupid hanging in mid-air. 'You told me to pretend—'

'You weren't serious?' he queried, his eyes silvering. 'I could have sworn.'

There were beads of sweat on his forehead and in the creases of his nose. She wanted to lick them, to taste the salt. Her tongue slipped out a little and she hastily retracted it.

'Are you crazy?' she cried defensively. But a little late.

Leo gave her a rueful smile and slid her down his body, then turned abruptly away. 'Probably,' came his muffled voice. 'What now? Shower? Swim? Arsenic sandwich?'

Ginny went for the first two and declined the third.

The swim kept them apart for a while. It seemed as if neither of them wanted to be alone with the other and they spent a pleasant if slightly uncomfortable time chatting to a group of fellow guests on the beach.

Later that morning Leo joined a small group on the hotel launch for a spot of scuba-diving off the impressive underwater cliffs formed by the slopes of the Piton mountains which ran straight into the sea.

When he'd gone, Ginny mooched about on the beach unable to settle. The people they'd been talking to earlier noticed her solitary wanderings up and down the shoreline and took pity on her, drawing her into their group and insisting that she join them for lunch in the beach bar.

Their gentle ribbing when she kept looking towards the headland where the hotel launch would first appear made her blush in confusion. But she joined in the laughter and enjoyed being with everyone—though their company only took the edge off Leo's absence. To her dismay, she missed him dreadfully.

Her heart leapt with joy when she saw him again and it was all she could do to keep herself on the beach lounger. Hastily she buried her head in her book, waiting while he disappeared into the diving shop to return the tanks and weights and to strip off his wetsuit.

'He's taking an awful long time,' she complained. She shifted, sat up and glanced up the beach. 'Not a sign of him!' People nearby were giggling and she flopped back with a rueful grin. 'OK, OK! So I've been like a dog waiting for its master,' she protested, good-naturedly poking fun at herself.

'It's been very sweet,' defended one of the older women. 'You really miss your husband's company!'

'Yes, I do,' confessed Ginny. 'I really do. Just don't tell him I can't survive without him when he comes back, will you? He'd be a bit unnerved to think I'm a lovesick idiot who can't manage a few hours without him!'

Gales of laughter floated across to her from all sides. It wasn't that funny. Puzzled, she looked about her and saw several pairs of eyes dart to... She stiffened. To someone evidently standing behind her.

Slowly she sat up again and swivelled around in the chair. Leo was smiling down at her, his expression one of tender adoration. Appalled, she had to suffer his warm kiss, the caress of his hand on her scarlet face, then force herself to laugh with the others at this evil, cruel trick.

'I think I fooled them! I made a good show of being lost without you, didn't I?' she murmured urgently in his ear.

He didn't look convinced that she'd been pretending. 'Terribly convincing,' he agreed softly. 'Almost fooled me for a moment.'

His velvety voice wrapped itself around her and she wished that she could be honest and tell him how much she still loved him. But where would that get them? He would cut her down to size and she'd be a snivelling wreck, no good for man nor beast and certainly not for work. And she still had the balance of her debt to pay back to the courts.

Ginny gave him a bright smile. 'I'm getting good at deception,' she said softly.

Leo lifted a sardonic eyebrow in agreement and raised his voice so that it would carry. 'I missed you so much, sweetheart,' he said consolingly as he sat down on her lounger and put his arm around her affectionately. He did his little-boy-bemused look for the smiling on-lookers. 'Sorry! Mustn't embarrass you... but we're madly, hopelessly in love,' he said helplessly to everyone, the epitome of an English gentleman who felt awkward with his emotions. 'Aren't we, darling?'

'Yes,' she croaked in dismay. For her it was true!

'Next time you must come with me,' he purred. 'I kept wanting to point things out to you. It was fantastic, Ginny! Spectacular. The coral is absolutely beautiful— and so many shapes you wouldn't believe!' he said with disarming enthusiasm.

'You know I'm scared of deep dives,' she said reluctantly. To any outsider he would have seemed genuinely excited and impatient to tell her everything he'd experienced. It was nothing but an act, and forcing herself to endure the bitter-sweet pretence was becoming a torture she'd rather do without.

'I know, darling.' He smiled sympathetically. 'I'd be with you every flap of your flipper.' Gently he kissed the tilt of her mouth when she let a wry smile escape. 'You'll be so intrigued you'll forget any fear. Do you know, there were shrimps there doing a car wash on an eel? It opened its mouth and they hoovered it out like a team of manic office cleaners ...'

Relaxing in his arms, she listened with the others to his enthusiastic descriptions—of forests of coral, yellow and purple tube sponges, crabs, sea lilies and basket stars, of chub and snapper and barjacks, dainty sea horses and the brilliantly coloured parrot fish.

And she found herself agreeing to start learning to scuba-dive from the beach so that she could accompany Leo when he went on the most spectacular event of all—a night dive, when the reef would really be 'alive'.

He went to find himself a lounger and they lay basking in the hot sunshine holding hands. Several times she was close to tears because it was such a lovely experience after the loneliness of the long, empty morning without him.

And when those moments of emotion came she must have tensed her body and transmitted her feelings, because each time Leo leant over, kissed her gently and squeezed her hand.

No words, no mockery, no intrusive probing. Just the kiss and the comfort of his big, safe hand. It was a very sensitive and perceptive response and she wanted nothing else. Awesome. Worrying.

That night she lay in the velvet darkness, listening to the marvellously tropical night sounds as thousands of tree frogs opened their throats and croaked rhythmically in the inky black jungle. The relaxation had been wonderful from one point of view because all her work-related stresses seemed to have disappeared.

But she felt too languid, too liquid-limbed. Her brain had stopped whirling, which was good, yet the frenetic muddle had been replaced by an insidious and all-pervasive knowledge that had settled in her mind like an uninvited guest.

She liked being with Leo, enjoyed his company, found him amusing and considerate and utterly irresistible. Her love hadn't been killed by his infidelity. It had only been suppressed by her pride and jealousy—and now it had returned even stronger than before.

Yet they were incompatible. Their relationship had nowhere to go. For Leo the pretence of being a loving husband was only a means to an end. Once he was sure that she wouldn't ruin the Brandon name by calling press attention to her association with the scandalous Vincente St Honoré, he'd be free to marry again.

Ginny gave a sob and muffled the sound with her pillow. She wanted him. She wanted Leo. If that had been all, she would have fought for him. But she didn't want the Brandon dynasty or Castlestowe and she knew that she couldn't compete with several hundred years of tradition and heritage.

'Crying, Ginny?'

Sounding only vaguely interested, he stood in her doorway, a candle in his hand. Half-naked except for a pair of shorts. Beautiful. *Why* couldn't she have him? It was so cruel of fate to put barriers in the way! The soft golden flicker from the candle played on the planes and valleys of his tanned torso, giving the satiny skin a sheen that demanded to be touched.

Ginny rolled over, hair dishevelled and falling over a face wet with tears, her clouded eyes yearning for him. He took a hesitant step into the room and she watched him, love and caution battling inside her. She had to be strong. She must send him away.

He held the candle outstretched, trying to see her face behind the gauzy mosquito net, her veil of hair. '*Were* you crying?' he asked again. Again offhand. Polite.

'No!' She spoilt her denial with a huge, shuddering sob that wrenched itself from deep inside her. Fool! she berated herself. He'd fall about laughing!

Leo didn't laugh. Solemnly he put the candle on a shelf, lifted the mosquito netting and sat down on the bed. When he reached out she closed her eyes, unable to bear the suspense. She felt his hand stroking her hair and snuffled more loudly.

'What's wrong?' he asked softly.

She smelt the warm, clean skin close and knew he must be leaning over her. Slowly her wet lashes lifted and he gave her a long, slow look that made her tremble so much that she took refuge by flinging her arms around his neck and burying her face in his bare chest.

'It's all this *waiting*!' she wailed. Her hands clung to his muscled shoulders like limpets and for a mad, reckless moment she wished that he'd be overwhelmed by her nearness and find her irresistible. He must know she always slept naked. He must be able to tell that there was nothing but a sheet between them.

'We've had... fun, haven't we?' he asked mildly.

Ginny sighed. Leo stroked her naked back, under the impression that it was soothing. Far from it. The drift of his fingers made her shiver in delicious pleasure, damn him!

Leo's skin tasted good to her slightly parted lips. He smelt so good. Felt even better. And she'd begun to ache in the deepest parts of her body. A suppressed groan rippled through her and quickly she flashed him a wary look to see if he'd noticed. Apparently not. He was already drawing away, his expression neutral.

She was resistible. That annoyed her. Wasn't she good enough for him? Men flung themselves at her feet! A voice in her head said cruelly, But not men of substance. Not men like Leo.

'I wish Vincente would get in touch! I can't stand hanging around!' she stormed angrily. 'Wasting time, fiddling around, playing the sweetly loving wife—it's nauseating!'

Leo studied her for a moment or two, maddening her with his inscrutable poker-face. 'I thought you wanted a little time to yourself?'

'It's too long!' she muttered. 'And you're driving me nuts with your slurpy husband stuff—'

'All right!' he interrupted sharply. 'Perhaps we've waited long enough for something to happen.'

Ginny looked up, puzzled. He sounded regretful. 'Don't you want me to clear this matter up?' she asked slowly.

Leo started, his eyes guarded. 'You mean with Vincente? Of course,' he said quickly. 'I'm not keen on you meeting him, but I see the necessity. I had no idea you hated having to be in my company so much. I thought . . .

'Well,' he said with a shrug of his shoulders, drawing further away from the white-faced Ginny, 'in that case we'd better flush Vincente out and to hell with the courtesy of waiting to be contacted by him when he feels up to it.'

'Oh!' The suddenness of the proposed action stopped her in her tracks. 'I was thinking of looking up the addresses and telephone numbers of the hospitals in the hotel phone book,' she said hesitantly, not knowing whether to be glad or sorry that they were taking action at last.

'We'll do that. We'll ring and find out which one he's in and if he's still too ill to see us.'

'What if he isn't up to coping with visitors?' she asked anxiously.

'I suggest we find Pascal, talk to him and see what we can learn.'

'He's hostile!' she protested. 'He rushed in here, demanding to know why I'd been asking for his father and insisting that I left at once! I don't think we'll get much out of him.'

'Don't you realise *why* he's hostile?' asked Leo quietly. She shook her head. 'You're a threat, Ginny. Vincente is a very wealthy man and at the moment Pascal presumably stands to inherit his whole fortune. A newly discovered sister would mean his inheritance is halved overnight. That's one of the reasons I've wanted to stay close to you. Pascal isn't to be trusted where you're concerned.'

Ginny was stunned. 'Surely you're not implying...?'

'I take no chances. We're talking really big money here, Ginny. And greed is one of the most dangerous of human sins.'

The thought of violence silenced her. Pascal had good reason to harm her. 'You'll stay with me, won't you?' she begged, her eyes wide with worry. 'Don't... I'd rather you didn't leave me alone again,' she mumbled, feeling horrified at her feebleness.

Something dark cut out the light in his eyes. 'If that's what you want. Till this is cleared up,' he said shortly.

Her mouth crimped at his reluctance. 'Yes, yes, of course,' Ginny agreed hastily. 'What if Vincente isn't in hospital at all? No one here seems to know where he lives—'

'Or, more likely, they're not prepared to tell us.'

She frowned. 'Why would that be?'

He shrugged. 'Something to do with his reputation... or Pascal—he might have told them you're intending to claim a relationship with his father...' Leo scowled. 'It seems so unlikely. He can't have primed *everyone* here. Every time I've made an enquiry, I've been met with stonewalling.'

'I know,' she said slowly. 'Me too. I get the impression that people are clamming up. Why? It worries me, Leo. Are people protecting him or themselves? Are they scared or merely hostile—to him or me?'

'I don't know,' admitted Leo. 'Beats me.' He smiled reassuringly at her. 'If we get no joy from the hospitals, I suggest a trip to Castries in the morning. We could have lunch and a look around, check out the library and pump anyone we can for information.'

'Sounds—' Just in time, Ginny stopped herself from saying that it sounded lovely. 'Sounds sensible,' she amended huskily.

His hand lay warm and comforting on her neck. 'I think you've waited long enough,' he drawled, his fingers idly lifting the soft, downy hairs at her nape and making her shiver with the delicious sensation.

Her starry eyes met his. 'I have,' she said, her voice shaking. He smiled faintly and her gaze drifted down to his beautifully chiselled mouth. 'Leo...' she began.

'Get some sleep,' he told her drily. 'It could be an emotional day for you.'

'What?' Her mind, her eyes, her body were all concentrated on his mouth. She remembered so well that arching of his upper lip. It had always meant that he was about to kiss her. Anticipation scurried through her veins.

'Vincente might turn out to be your father,' he said gravely. 'That could change your life.'

'Uh-huh.'

It didn't interest her as much as it should have done. Leo occupied her mind and everything else seemed far away and relatively unimportant. Imperceptibly, she moved closer to him and the sheet fell away. Incredibly, she didn't care. For a brief second or two he looked down at the softly lifting globes of her breasts. His lips parted to show his even white teeth and every sinew in her body tautened like whipcord with the expectation of feeling the softness of his mouth encircling each hard, plum-dark nipple.

'Ginny...' His voice thrilled her. It was thick with desire.

'Yes. Please,' she whispered, trailing her fingers through his hair, affectionately pushing back the dark wave that had dipped on his forehead.

'You know I can't. Nice of you to offer. But I'm waiting for the woman who won't fit me into her busy schedule only when it suits her.'

The rebuke in the words whipped her like a lash. Tempting though she was to a red-blooded man like Leo, however available and willing she might be, he was choosing to wait for Miss Suitable back home. 'Leo!' she croaked in reproach.

He wilted her with an icy glare. 'Forget the studied allure of limpid eyes and pouting lips! I don't come running when women snap their fingers because they're hungry for a night's entertainment,' he growled. 'Try getting your thrills from one of your magazine covers,' he added scathingly.

Ginny was stunned by his vicious tone and his uncharacteristic spitefulness. 'That's petty of you, Leo!' she said bitterly.

'No. That's wisdom,' he said tightly. 'I'm not leaping into bed with you in the heat of the moment. Sex on its own has never been enough for me. I want the emotions that go hand in hand with commitment—'

'Like with Arabella?' she flung defiantly at him.

'You fool,' he said quietly, his eyes dark and glittering. 'You stupid *fool*! Arabella is beautiful, empty and shallow. Money is her god. Money and fame. She's no more capable of real commitment than you were!'

'Then why—?'

'Whey did you find us in bed together?' he asked harshly.

Ginny winced. 'Yes!'

'When you've worked that out,' he gritted, 'you might be halfway to understanding me. Goodnight.'

Confused, and humiliated by his contempt for her, she clamped her mouth shut and sullenly watched him walking away. His words had hurt her. But then truth often did.

Rigid with misery, she waited till his door had shut, rolled over mournfully and let the air collapse out of her lungs. Limp and listless, she stared into space, waiting for the dawn. And this time she wished that Leo would leave her to the mercies of Vincente and Pascal St Honoré. They might be dangerous men, but Leo was lethal. Everything she did must be aimed at finding Vincente, establishing whether there was any relationship between them, and getting Leo out of her life for good.

And no crying! she told herself, gritting her teeth against the seeping tears. Now was the time to stand on her own feet and dismiss all hope of finding a solution to her heartfelt desire—that she and Leo could somehow, anyhow, live together in love and harmony.

His opinion of her was too low. And the eventual heir to the earldom would never remarry a woman he thought to be a fool and promiscuous. She had to retreat again into cool indifference, and perhaps, if he hated her even more, he'd feel less inclined to be civil. Castries tomorrow. Maybe two, three days at the most before she could be free of Leo.

Horror filled her with its cold claws and she hugged herself tightly for comfort, rocking like a child in the big double bed. Then some pride, some strength returned to her and she tossed back her hair in a grim gesture. She'd managed before. Why not again? *Because she didn't want to,* came the reply. And it was a while before she pushed that aside and found her composure again.

CHAPTER SIX

AMAZINGLY, Leo behaved the next morning as if nothing had happened. Perhaps he looked a little tired, his carved mouth a little less firm, the smoky eyes half-hidden by thick, silky lashes, as though he'd slept as little as she. And perhaps his bearing was a little stiff, instead of full of that elegant looseness that came from striding around his own land.

Still, she had to admit that he was courtesy itself. Whereas Ginny felt exhausted and subdued, dreading the day in Castries, and clawing back her old barriers against the world to hide behind during the long hours she would be spending with Leo and his fatal charm.

Wearing a divided skirt that swirled around her long, slender legs, and with a big Bagshaw shirt over a white cropped top—the first concealing, the second revealing her body—she stepped nervously into the hotel launch.

'Take my hand, darling,' murmured Leo. The voice was warm, the hand cold, with a stranger's politeness.

She did so, with a brief, cool acknowledgement so that he got the message. Go too far in the darling mode and you'll end up overboard, the message said. Her heart sighed for the days when he would have caught her in his arms and whirled her around, laughing. Taken any excuse to touch her. Their hands had entwined, their eyes had constantly met and lingered . . .

'Hey, welcome again!' The man standing behind the

wheel grinned at Leo. 'You like Castries so much last time, you bring your wife?'

Leo stiffened imperceptibly at her side but it was enough for her to notice. 'You're mistaking me for someone else...er...Joseph,' he said, checking the man's name-tag. 'Some other guy.'

'Oh, sure.' Joseph grinned with a knowing wink. 'I get you! First trip, eh? Enjoy!'

A mistake. Ginny relaxed. And she was so occupied with her image of cool detachment that she thought no more of Leo's reaction. With so many hotel guests taking advantage of the taxi service to Castries, it must be easy to be confused.

The launch eased out of the bay, careful not to damage the fragile coral. Once they were out to sea, Joseph opened the throttle and she lifted her face to the rush of air and spray, revelling in the speed and sense of freedom. A sudden shower of tropical rain was driven by a head wind onto their unprotected bodies, but nobody minded, least of all Ginny, who crammed her hair under a baseball cap and watched with pleasure as the double rainbows split the skies with breathtaking arcs of colour.

To the north of the hotel bay lay enticing coves, the small crescents of deserted beaches backed by coconut palms and with the occasional flame-tree standing like a tall orange beacon in a sea of green rainforest.

'That's so romantic!' Ginny yelled to Joseph. She pointed to a sweep of sand between two headlands, the palms so dense that the mysterious darkness beneath them seemed almost sinister.

Joseph nodded. 'Beau Rivage. It's—'

'Look! Is that a dolphin?' cried Leo suddenly.

Ginny and the other two couples on the boat rushed to the seaward side, all interest in the coastline forgotten till they decided that Leo had been mistaken, though Ginny was the last to accept that he could have made an error of judgement; it was just so out of character. Still, she thought, shrugging off the incident, who was she to think she knew him well?

She liked Castries. Before, in the madness of a photographic shoot, it had seemed hot and shabby. Now it appealed to her desire for things that weren't glossy on the surface but which had more substance.

Castries certainly had a soul and a heartbeat. Far from being a tourist centre with touristy shops and rip-off merchants, it had an independent life of its own, a vibrancy that made it almost hum with activity.

The small harbour was busy with ships being loaded with bananas and citrus fruit. Glamour was provided by several schooners with furled sails being provisioned for romantic journeys on the high seas. Terribly exciting! She felt fizzy with anticipation, as if she'd drunk a bottle of champagne and was floating on the bubbles, and it was hard to remain cool when she wanted to chatter away about everything she saw.

Declining Leo's imperiously offered arm, she walked with him from the dock. The streets were packed with people, the roads full of slow-moving cars and trucks and minibuses, all virtually bouncing with the beat of music from within.

'This way,' said Leo confidently, after a cursory look at the street map.

'Jeremie Street. I remember it,' she said with pleasure. 'I did a shoot here.' They paused among the brightly dressed traders who sat cross-legged on both pavements of the street for as far as the eye could see. Ginny's eyes widened at the heaps of exotic fruits and vegetables piled in front of them in a kaleidoscope of colour. Chaos reigned. A lovely, jolly chaos.

'It wasn't easy getting the shots we wanted,' she said wryly, remembering the arguments and the bad temper when the St Lucians had refused to move their pitches and the traffic had refused to stop. 'We were rather a nuisance.'

'I can imagine.' Leo made a face. 'You must have behaved like aliens. Nicer to be a normal sightseer, isn't it?' he said slyly.

It was—but she'd never admit that. Nicer to be unknown, free to wander around without people staring in that blank, slightly hostile way. Finding herself smiling sentimentally, she said briskly, 'That's neither here nor there. Where's the library?'

'Not far. We're going in the right direction. Let me soak up a little of the atmosphere for a moment longer,' said Leo persuasively. 'It's fascinating.'

The noise, the bustle and sheer exuberance that lifted from the jam-packed pavements drew Ginny like a magnet. It would have been lovely to stay longer, to ask what some of the strange fruits were, to play the carefree tourist. But she'd be a fool if she fell into the trap of enjoying herself with Leo again—or wasting time, as he seemed determined to do.

'If you like it that much, you can return here on your own,' she said firmly, snatching the map from his hand. 'Or stay and wallow in the atmosphere now, while I find the library myself. Columbus Square. Fine. See you later—'

'No!' He caught her arm forcefully. 'We do this together. You're not trotting around this town on your own.'

She heaved an impatient sigh. 'If you insist, but let's get on with it,' she said coldly. Her eyes narrowed. 'But would you mind taking your hand away? And don't grab me like that again. I'm not in the mood for playing shepherd and sheep.'

'Angry because I turned you down last night?' he drawled, ignoring her request and pulling her to him. The chiselled bow of his mouth lifted sardonically. 'Pettiness, wouldn't you say?'

'Not at all!' she snapped back. 'Last night I was worried and upset and in need of comfort and you jumped to the conclusion that I was after your body.'

Ginny dragged in a rather shaky breath. The lie wasn't coming easily. Something to do with having her body touching his so intimately. He felt warm. Male. Intoxicating...

'I don't want you making the same mistake again,' she went on harshly, ignoring the weakening effect of the lure of his parted lips. Calculating brute! He was hoping that she'd fall feebly at his feet. But she wouldn't be dominated!

'Did I really make a mistake?' he asked in soft disbelief.

Ginny wondered how much he knew of her liquefaction. If she hadn't been gripping his shoulders tightly, she might have melted into him, she thought moodily.

'Men have the habit of misinterpreting women's signals,' she tossed in a snappy, no-nonsense manner.

'You're no exception. So I will make my feelings clearer in future.'

Leo nodded, assessing the tension in her body with a casual sweep of his smoky eyes. And he gave an infuriating little chuckle, narrowing the circle of his enclosing arms. 'They're clearer by the minute.'

She felt the temperature rising between them. Was that all *her*? Were her palms sweating because of his heat— or hers? Or both... 'What's that meant to mean?' she asked belligerently, afraid that she was betraying herself. He'd feel the heat coming off her. What would he make of it?

His linked hands pressed into the small of her back, driving her pelvis closer to his, and she resisted with all her strength. 'I do believe you are getting...' His pause had her holding her breath. Did he know? She went scarlet with mortification. 'Annoyed,' he said finally, his mouth curving in amusement when she let out a sharp breath of relief. 'Annoyed with me, or yourself, I wonder?'

Her eyes said that she was close to exploding. So did her prim mouth, the pressure of her hands on his shoulders as she fought to keep a decent distance between them. The rest of her was telling another story and she knew from the mockery in his cynical grey eyes that he'd realised that. She had to break free. With dignity.

'Are you going to let me go or do I treat you to a résumé of my expensive self-defence lessons and then scream loudly for help?' Her head tipped back and she looked down her nose haughtily at him. 'I don't want you hanging onto me while we walk around this town—'

'But, darling,' he reproached in mock affection, 'holding hands would be normal for a happily married couple like us. We really can't march angrily along like cross children on their way to find teacher.'

Ginny's eyes blazed. Cross children indeed! 'Stop being so damned patronising! Nobody knows us in Castries!' she seethed. 'Stop this *farce* of togetherness!'

'Sweetheart,' he murmured soothingly, 'we know for a fact that there are two couples from the hotel wandering around. Perhaps others. Maybe Vincente is out of hospital and doing a little light shopping. Or Pascal is knocking back Planter's Punches in a friendly neighbourhood bar. We've no idea—'

'It's very unlikely,' she snapped. His face had bent close to hers. Tanned and smooth, maddeningly kissable. In her mind she could almost feel the satin slide of his skin over her soft lips. Sharp and swift came a spasm of need in response to the thought. And she was hanging onto her dignity and her pride by a slender thread while her eyes and her mouth must have been revealing her desire and her pelvis strained against her will power in an effort to break that thread.

'Unlikely, but possible. While there's the chance we'll be seen we must keep the farce going,' he said reasonably, toying with a lock of hair blowing across her face. He tucked it behind her ear. Slowly. He knew how sensitive her ears were! she thought angrily, gritting her teeth. Delicious tremors were chasing up and down her chest. She swayed on her feet and he smiled winningly at her. 'I know it's not very funny and neither of us can stand the sight of each other,' he murmured, apparently blind to the way she felt, 'but it suits my purpose and it suits yours.'

'No, it doesn't!' she insisted hotly. Too hotly. Taking slow, deep breaths, she struggled to get herself calmer. 'OK, we're supposed to be married and...and we're supposed to be mad about one another,' she said with difficulty. Her voice tightened with bitterness. 'People in love don't always have to be grabbing each other—'

'Yes, they do.' Leo's voice was low and husky and it vibrated into every corner of her yearning body. 'Lovers are impelled to touch one another,' he said silkily. 'Half the time they don't even know they're doing it.'

Her mental powers seemed to be at a standstill. In a daze she felt his hands unclasp at the dip of her waist. His palms moved tantalisingly up her back beneath the loose shirt, coming to rest on her naked flesh between the cropped top and her skirt.

She exhaled very slowly, steeling herself to resist. 'Don't *do* that!' she muttered, twisting away from him. Attack was better than defence.

Standing there, panting a little and wanting to hurl herself headlong into his arms, she had a brainwave that would save her. 'You know, Leo,' she said thoughtfully, with only a slight tremor in her voice, 'if I didn't know better I'd be wondering why *you* have to keep touching *me*.' At his indrawn breath, she stretched her long, slender neck and met his ash-pale eyes boldly. 'Not still in love with me, are you?' she scathed, hurting herself with the question. Pigs might fly! she thought bitterly.

The ash-coloured eyes smouldered and ignited into white fire. 'I'm trying to protect my family from scandal. You know why I'm pretending we're still married.'

'The Brandon name!' she muttered bitterly.

'The Brandon name,' he agreed in a low voice. 'The combination of you and Vincente is potentially damaging. I don't want to touch you,' he growled, 'but sometimes...' His mouth twisted wryly. 'Sometimes I have to,' he finished softly.

Ginny winced. He had to because he wanted to keep her in order. She had to touch *him* because she found it impossible to keep her hands off him. 'The trouble with you is,' she said frostily, 'you're too used to lording it over everyone at Castlestowe.'

That wasn't strictly correct and she knew it. He had a kind of family relationship with the staff there—maybe because he'd grown up with them all. But the taunt suited her purpose.

'If that's how you see it,' he said quietly, 'you're even less perceptive than I thought.' And Ginny winced, her jibe backfiring on her. 'Incidentally,' he added casually, 'there's a hell of a crowd up Laborie Street by the looks of it. Take my arm and we'll forge through together.'

'No, thanks. We'll do better on our own,' she said stubbornly.

And she regretted her decision almost immediately. Everyone seemed to be flowing down the street in a fast, unstoppable tide, and they were swimming against it. Over and over again she was knocked, bumped and jostled. People weren't hostile and they apologised with friendly grins, but she felt relieved when they were in the less congested square.

Aware that Leo was eyeing her with an 'I told you so' expression on his smirking face, she pretended not to notice and scanned the buildings anxiously for some sign to tell her which one the library was.

'It's the one on the corner,' he offered in amusement.

With a haughty angling of her head, she strode with determination towards the once beautiful old colonial building and climbed the steps inside to the reference room. This should end the ridiculous charade that she and Leo were playing. After her visit here, life would be considerably less complicated.

Though, judging from the flaking paint everywhere, the limited number of books and their old-fashioned bindings, she might come away disappointed. Dismayed, she studied the earnest readers, apparently content with their lot. 'Where do we start?' she whispered.

'You find somewhere for us to sit,' murmured Leo. 'I'll chat up the librarian and see what she can suggest.'

He gave her a gentle shove towards the tables which took up most of the room and she edged around them to a couple of chairs. Not surprisingly, the librarian quickly succumbed to Leo's neon charm and chatted away merrily, lifting three reference books and a directory from a stack behind her. Even from fifteen feet Ginny could see that the books were dilapidated and held together with sticky tape but Leo bore them over to her as though they were the crown jewels.

'This is all, apparently,' he said in an undertone, passing her the books.

'You're joking!'

'No. If the information isn't in there, it isn't anywhere.' He beamed at her encouragingly. 'You go through them and I'll check the telephone directory.'

There was a silence for a while and then, to her amazement, he said, 'Well, that's that. Nothing in here under St Honoré.' Before she could make any comment, he'd slipped from his chair and returned the book to the librarian.

'Nothing?' she whispered with a frown when he returned. 'There must be!'

'Unless he's ex-directory,' he suggested glibly. 'You know how it is with wealthy people.' Her face still expressed doubt. 'Any luck your end?' he asked with an innocent interest.

Ginny was instantly on her guard. Leo, innocent? He was playing some devious game, judging by the look in his eye. She wondered what, and why. 'These books are worse than useless,' she muttered. 'All I've discovered is that St Honoré was given land near Soufrière by Louis XVI in 1784. That's it.'

'It's a start,' he said brightly.

Ginny gave him a scathing glance. 'It's nothing of the kind. These books aren't exactly up to date, Leo.' Her long fingers found the date in a collapsing volume. 'This was published in 1920. That one…1897, this one…1935.' Her angry eyes accused him. 'Are you quite certain that there aren't any more books we can look at?' she asked coldly.

'Have a look around,' said Leo with a shrug that dissociated him from any blame. 'It's not generously supplied, is it?' Accidentally, his warm knee gently connected with hers. The shock travelled through her body, leaving her a quivering mess and wanting more. 'We've drawn a blank, I'm afraid. What a shame. Shall we go?' he suggested sympathetically.

Somehow Ginny pulled herself together, despite the fact that his face was hovering close to hers while he whispered to her intimately and his eyes were warm and indulgent. 'There must be something here—'

'Tell you what,' he said smoothly. 'I could try the post office in Bridge Street while you check out the shops there.'

She looked up and tried to ignore the persuasive smile. 'You're remarkably clued up on the amenities,' she said, puzzled.

'I'm good at maps,' he replied. 'Apparently there's a good restaurant in the same street. What about a long lunch and a stroll in the sunshine? A little duty-free shopping in the complex, collect a few souvenirs, check out the boutiques...' He angled his head appealingly.

It was all too appealing. He seemed genuinely sorry, sporting a big, generous smile and a friendly, compassionate expression as if he knew how disappointed she was. Miserably she wondered if he was deliberately coaxing her away so that she left without the information she needed. She knew what she had to do: search all the shelves in the library if necessary, pester the librarian till she got a lead on Vincente. Hermit or not, he couldn't have disappeared totally.

But she would have loved to spend the rest of the day mooching about with Leo. Ginny's long lashes lowered to cover the wistfulness in her eyes. All her life seemed to be one big, long denial—of her emotions, of food, of a need to spend quality time on herself. And now she was having to deny herself one afternoon in Leo's company.

No long lunch. No stroll in the sunshine. No lazy day in the sunshine. She had something to do and she mustn't let him coax her out of it. It was for the best, she told herself ruthlessly. He'd walk all over her if she took the easy way out.

'Do whatever you want,' she said quietly. 'I'm going to look for clues here myself. You see, Leo, I don't trust you.' Slipping from her chair, she turned to the shelves behind them. Knowing nothing about the organisation of books in a reference library, she gave a cursory glance to the titles, hoping to find the history section. Or maybe—

'Hello again!' said a soft voice behind her. Hearing Leo's stifled exclamation of dismay, she turned her head to find a young man smiling good-naturedly at him. 'Didn't you find what you wanted the other day?' the young man asked.

Leo stood up slowly, his eyes narrowing as he struggled to think of a reply. 'N-no,' was all he managed.

Ginny drew in a sharp breath. Leo had been here before! Furious, she glared at him intently while he exchanged a few desultory remarks with the young man. After a moment the two of them shook hands and the young man left. Leo sat down and pretended to be engrossed in the economic history of St Lucia.

Shaking with anger, she slid into the chair opposite him, reached out, flipped the book shut and snatched it away. 'You rat!' she whispered furiously. 'You've been here before!'

'Yup.' He met her eyes, his expression guarded.

'And you're hiding something from me!' she accused.

His hands opened in a gesture of admission. 'True.'

Her mouth dropped open at his gall. 'And what,' she snapped frostily, 'might that be? An address, perhaps? Vincente's address?'

'Yes.'

People were looking at them curiously. Ginny offered around a few apologetic looks and kept her voice low.

'You are a mean, dirty, underhand little worm,' she said, growling each word out in tight anger. 'And you will stop fobbing me off with useless books and making a fool out of me and lead me to the information *now*.'

And to her relief he nodded with a heavy reluctance. 'All right. Have it your own way. I agree.' He unravelled his long legs and rose, not at all abashed, but oozing authority and command. 'Come with me.'

Incoherent with rage, Ginny followed him, but instead of going to a book stack or to the reference desk he walked outside and began to hurry down the steps. After a moment of stunned surprise, she ran after him.

'Where are you going?' she yelled, her voice echoing down the bare stairway.

'You want the information—it's this way,' he called back grumpily over his shoulder.

'If this is a trick...!' she yelled, her hair flying as she stormed after him.

. 'No trick. Trust me.'

'*Trust* you?' Outside, she rounded on him, her body tight with fury. 'Why ever should I do that? You've been manipulating me ever since you arrived, you unspeakable rat!' she raged. 'You knew! You knew where Vincente lived! You could have told me *ages* ago, instead of making me go through this ridiculous play-acting with you! When I think of the lies, the prevarications, the downright ruthless way you kept the information to yourself, I feel...I feel... Oh, I could tear my nails down your face, you vicious, spiteful brute! How dare you play God? Why, Leo, why? Go on, tell me it was for my own good!'

'It was for your own good,' drawled Leo obligingly.

'It isn't *funny*!' she cried, her eyes as dark as black honey with anger. 'You must have known for *days*! And you pretended that I must wait, so I sat around like a lemon, wasting time. Oh-h-h!' she spluttered. 'I didn't have to suffer that ghastly married stuff at all! You could have taken me straight to where Vincente lives—'

'You've had your say; now listen to me!' Leo said curtly, shaking her by the shoulders. 'Dammit, listen! Doesn't it occur to you that I might have had a reason?'

'Yes,' she muttered bitterly, her mouth sulky with resentment. 'Revenge. You wanted to give me a bad time. You liked to think I was in your power, dancing to your tune! And you're scared stiff that the press will associate me with Vincente and your wretched family will get the backwash of his reputation. That's ridiculous!' she scathed. 'No one could blame the Brandons for bad judgement—'

'What do you mean by that?' he snarled.

Ginny's eyes glittered. 'Your unfortunate marriage to me—a shallow, materialistic model who's a cheap little opportunist,' she said bitterly. 'And my possible relationship to a lecherous middle-aged man in the West Indies. It would make a good story, I can see. All the past rumours about me being a tramp would be instantly confirmed in everyone's eyes if a man with Vincente's reputation was discovered to be my father!'

Her voice was shaking. She stopped for a moment to control it but the situation was too horrible for her to cope with. In despair she lifted her fists and battered his chest furiously. Leo just stood there, letting her. And then the waves of hopelessness engulfed her and she let her hands fall limply to her sides.

'I hope you're thinking straight now,' he growled. 'You could do untold damage to *your* reputation, as well as the Brandons'. Walk away from it, Ginny, before it's too late!'

'How can I? I can't turn my back on a question mark in my life, however unpleasant the answer might be. I have a lifetime habit of facing up to things, Leo,' she said grimly. 'So you can forget your manipulative little game! This is my business. You have no right to interfere. Not any more. Start talking—and no more lies!'

'Oh, you'll get the whole story,' he growled. 'But not here in the street. You're drawing too much attention to us as it is. Over lunch.'

'Bother lunch!' she defied, resisting his urging hand on her elbow. 'Just give me the address and let me get on with it.' Fuming, she planted her hands on her hips in a grim challenge. 'Tell me—then I won't have to see you or speak to you again!'

'Is that what you want?' he asked flatly.

Her eyes closed as a spasm of pain razored through her. *'Yes!'* she rasped, emotion intensifying the force behind the word. And before she weakened she tilted up her chin and met his unreadable eyes straight on. 'Yes, yes, yes!' she hissed furiously, her voice rising in hysteria.

Leo studied her, his face a mask. 'Then you have to allow me to tell you in my own way,' he said tightly. 'I'm going to have lunch now. You can join me or not; it's your choice.'

'I don't need to,' she grated. 'I'm sure that information is in the library and you found it the first time you came here—'

'But it will take you a while to find and if you don't listen to me you'll never learn the details. You won't find out why I'm so hostile to Vincente, for instance. It's more than a fear of scandal, I can assure you. If you wish to remain in ignorance of his wife, that's your funeral. You can do as you damn well please.'

'His . . . wife?' she asked, bewildered. Ginny trembled at the brief flash of pity in his eyes and her heart began to thud violently. What did he know? 'Do you mean my mother? Could she be my mother?' she asked urgently, tugging at his arm.

Frowning, he contemptuously picked her fingers off one by one. 'We do this my way,' he said in a lordly manner. 'Lunch.'

Sullenly she watched him turn and walk off down the street, vowing she'd rather *die* than . . . What was wrong about the way he was walking? Her back went rigid. There was something about his manner that betrayed tension—perhaps the lifted shoulders, or the stiff and unnatural way he held his head.

Alarmed, Ginny wove in and out of the crowds, annoyed that she was being forced to run after him again, annoyed with herself for ever trusting him. He held the whip hand again. It seemed that he always would.

Suddenly he dived into a doorway and she hastened to catch up with him. It was a restaurant. Numb with apprehension, she stumbled up the stairs.

From the start Leo had tried to prevent her from seeking Vincente out, feeding her with terrible stories. Could she believe him now? He might dish out a load of lies and she'd be none the wiser. Whatever he said, it would make no difference. One way or another she'd have to meet Vincente and make up her own mind— and, remembering what Leo had said about Vincente's character, she cringed at the thought of doing that alone.

'Over here,' he called imperiously, making himself heard above a milling throng. Height and an aristocratic manner had its advantages! Outwardly calm now, she wriggled around the tables in the busy room and emerged on a balcony outside, overlooking a busy street. Leo was already sitting at a table and he stood briefly while she settled herself just as a waitress appeared by his side. 'Two rum punches,' he ordered abruptly. 'And a menu.'

'I don't want to drink or eat...' Ginny began fretfully.

'You will.' Leo's eyes were unusually dark, his face very solemn, and she shivered with fear.

'Why?' she husked. 'What is so awful? Why did you go to such lengths to set up an elaborate scenario where I was handed useless books by a primed, suitably dazzled librarian?'

With a sigh, he put a gentle hand on her shoulder. Irrationally, she drew strength from the gesture, reassured by its firm security. 'I thought I could stop you ever meeting Vincente,' he said quietly. 'The hotel staff were obviously keeping their own counsel about the man's whereabouts for reasons I can only guess at. I imagined you'd give up trying when we had no joy in the library—'

'I would have gone to the police station,' she said hoarsely, cold shivers running down her erect back in icy waves.

'And I would have thought of something to stop you.' Leo removed his hand and brooded moodily on the complex weave of the raffia mat. 'Faked a twisted ankle, developed stomach cramps—I don't know. Anything to get you back to the hotel and buy time till I could persuade you that you were wasting your time looking for

Vincente.' He grimaced. 'I didn't bargain on being recognised by anyone.'

'You're very striking,' she muttered. Her eyes flicked up quickly because she was anxious that he shouldn't imagine that she found him anything special. 'Tall,' she said curtly.

He acknowledged the arrival of their drinks and slid hers towards her. 'Take a few good swigs of that,' he ordered. 'Stop slicing me in half with your beautiful eyes and calm down. You've got to cope with a lot of information and some of it may make your hair stand on end.' Morosely he took a long gulp of his drink while Ginny sat in petrified silence, her lips parted in dismay. 'Drink,' he commanded roughly. 'I want you to be a little more mellow before I begin.'

With shaking hands, she held the glass and obediently took several swallows. The menu arrived and she stared at it blindly.

'Choose something,' he muttered.

'I can't... I—'

'You will eat,' he said brutally. 'I won't talk until you've got some food into you.'

'Damn you! *Damn you!* Why don't you get out of my life?' she half sobbed under her breath.

'I can't,' he snarled. 'I wish I could, but I can't. Not yet. Now choose something to eat.'

The list of food on the menu swam before her eyes. Somehow she forced herself to focus. Around her and inside the room beyond she became conscious of much laughter and barracking, as locals recognised one another and caught up with the gossip. In a time capsule of her own—one that was probably about to explode—Ginny read and reread the menu. European, Creole and South-

East Asian food. Thai shrimp rolls, she read for the third time. Java fish. Steak teriyaki.

'I don't know,' she muttered miserably. 'Anything...' She flinched at his sharply indrawn breath. 'Beef *rôti* and chilli sauce!' she said quickly.

They sat in an ominous silence till he ordered. Seafood and fish in black bean sauce for him. Ginny felt the worry and misery wrapping around her like a thick cloak. Any other time she would have loved the restaurant. It was unpretentious—unlike the stiff, expensive place they'd eaten at before on the shoot—and everyone appeared to be having a wonderful time.

On a small notice-board were adverts for local services. A step class. A beauty centre. Skin care, batik, a health club... Plenty going on. If it hadn't been for Vincente and Leo, she would have had fun here, she thought mournfully. St Lucia was her sort of place, the St Lucians her sort of people. None of them had 'attitude'. Not like Leo.

'Well?' she muttered when her meal finally arrived and she'd pushed down two—admittedly delicious—mouthfuls.

'Don't give me indigestion,' he said tetchily. 'I *am* going to tell you!' he growled, when she drew in a furious breath. 'Let me get something down me first.'

More drinks arrived. Ginny was beginning to feel anaesthetised. 'OK. I'm calm,' she said coldly, finishing the last of the *rôti*. It sat heavily in her stomach, but she was fuelled up and he couldn't delay any longer. 'Fulfil a promise for once in your life, will you?'

Leo pushed his plate away and she noticed suddenly that he'd eaten virtually nothing. 'First,' he said abruptly, 'Vincente isn't in hospital any longer. He's at home—'

'Which is where?' she asked quickly in an angry rasp.

'Beau Rivage.'

Ginny's mouth pinched in. 'Beau Rivage where the dolphins play offshore?' she asked sarcastically. Two high spots of colour burned in his cheeks but he stared back at her boldly. 'There was no dolphin, was there? You're such a liar! I despise you!' she said hotly, and she half rose to her feet before he brought her crashing down again by slamming a ruthless hand on each shoulder. 'What the—?'

'I haven't finished,' he growled. 'Sit there till I'm done!'

'You've got ten seconds,' she hissed, her eyes blistering his with an uncontrollable anger. 'And then I'm going!'

'Ten seconds will do. Vincente's wife was—is—my aunt.'

Ginny was too stunned to do anything but blink stupidly. 'Aunt?' she repeated, checking to see if it was some kind of joke. The strain in every line of his face told her that he was deadly serious.

'My father's sister.'

'Oh! The scandal...' She swallowed, remembering the woman whom, Leo had claimed, Vincente had treated badly. But was that true too? 'Leo!' she whispered. 'Tell me you're lying again!'

'Unfortunately not. Mary Brandon was my father's elder sister. Lady Mary Brandon,' he said in an almost clinical monotone, and Ginny tried to grasp the significance of what he was saying.

She looked up at his austere, bleak face and shivered despite the warmth on the small balcony. He looked very much like his father at that moment.

Stuart, Viscount Brandon, had always unnerved her with his aristocratic confidence. The fact that his family had for centuries owned vast tracts of land and moved in a close and intimate social circle meant that the red-haired Stuart had a very definite idea of who he was and where he was going. One day he'd be the Earl of Castlestowe. And then, in time to come, it would be Leo's turn.

The thought of that had intimidated her ever since she'd first realised Leo's destiny—but by then it had been too late. She'd fallen in love and stupidly imagined that love could conquer anything.

No wonder Leo had scorned the possibility that she might be Vincente's daughter. That would mean that Mary—*Lady* Mary—would be her mother. 'You said...you always looked after your own.'

'Yes.'

'Does that mean that your aunt was cared for by your father and grandfather when she left Vincente and fled to Britain?'

Leo frowned. 'By my father.'

Ginny heaved a sigh. Mary, Lady Brandon couldn't possibly be her mother, then. Because her mother had been poor and desperate, not cherished and protected by one of the richest men in Scotland. 'I'm not Vincente's daughter,' she said shakily.

He hesitated. 'I've always told you—it's highly unlikely.'

But that hesitation had put her on the alert. Leo wasn't telling her everything. Maybe not even the truth. 'There's a little more for me to know, isn't there?' she asked.

He frowned. 'Family business.'

Ginny squared her shoulders. 'If you want me to abandon this search for Vincente, you'd better tell me everything,' she said sharply.

His mouth thinned, as though it was painful telling anyone about a hiccup in the Brandon genealogy. 'You've been hunting down the biggest rogue you'll ever meet,' he grated. 'The kind of man who'd cheat his own cousin. There's a cloud hanging over that family, Ginny. You see, Vincente's cousin Louis died under suspicious circumstances. So did Pascal's first wife and baby son. They died in a fire. Vincente was implicated in both events—and Pascal was so certain that his father caused the fire that they had a brawl which resulted in Pascal going to prison for criminal damage and actual bodily harm.'

Ginny swallowed. What a family! If Leo could prove without a shadow of doubt that she couldn't be Mary's daughter, she'd be heartily relieved. 'Tell me about your aunt,' she said huskily. 'How did she meet Vincente?'

'Socially, in London. She was seventeen. Headstrong, stubborn, confident.' Leo's mouth twisted wryly. 'Apparently it was her engagement party. She was to marry Vincente's cousin Louis—a brilliant match, approved by everyone. Then, out of the blue, she declared this undying love for Vincente and they ran away to St Lucia. Gradually the family lost all contact with her and she even stopped writing to Father—who'd been a great friend as well as a brother to her.'

'Didn't anyone come over to find her?' she asked hesitantly.

'Several times. However, Vincente and Mary never seemed to be at home. Grandfather learnt of Pascal's birth from a local boatman.'

'That's terrible!' she said indignantly.

Leo shrugged. 'She'd cut herself off from the family. The Brandons are too proud to run after anyone.'

Ginny nodded soberly. She knew that only too well. 'So why should Vincente have thought for one moment that I might be their daughter? And how did he find out about my mother's name and my date of birth?'

'After thirteen years married to Vincente,' continued Leo patiently, 'she got in touch with Father out of the blue and begged him to help her leave the island.'

'Why?' breathed Ginny, unable to tear her eyes from his pale, tight face and his lowered eyes. A terrible sadness washed through her body and, desperate for Leo's touch, she reached out hesitantly with her slender hand and rested it on his, shocked to find that it was shaking because he was clenching it as if crushing the life from Vincente's neck. 'Was she unhappy?'

Leo fixed her with a piercing look. 'You have to stay away from the man,' he said tightly. 'My aunt suffered from Vincente's vile behaviour. He humiliated her by openly flaunting his mistresses. I understand that he attacked her, verbally and physically.' Leo's brows met in an angry line. 'He moved one of his mistresses into the house. That was when she decided to run away,' he muttered, and looked at her with such raw and bitter eyes that her heart lurched for him.

'She *was* the woman in the scandal!' she breathed in compassion. 'Why didn't she run away before?'

'She couldn't. Vincente's treatment had crushed her so much that she was terrified of stepping out of the house,' replied Leo grimly. 'Agoraphobia, I believe. She was a prisoner of her own mind. It took Father hours to persuade her to leave, once he reached her.'

'She must have been terrified,' Ginny said quietly. 'Leo, I'm so sorry.' Her hand tightened on his in sympathy.

'You do see what a terrible man Vincente is, don't you?' he asked urgently.

'Yes. Yes, I do.' Vincente was a brute. Thank heavens Leo had kept her away from the man! She tried to swallow away the lump in her throat as the sun slanted beneath the shady roof of the balcony and lit Leo's haunted face with a searing light. 'Your aunt,' she said gently. 'Is she all right now?'

Again that hesitation. Ginny tensed. He was about to lie to her.

'Leo, I want the truth,' she said, her voice hardening in warning. 'I deserve the truth. I can find out when I get back to England what happened to her—'

'Yes.' It was clear that Leo felt reluctant to tell her what he knew. Ginny waited while he stared sightlessly at the cheerful crowds below. 'I don't know,' he said slowly. His mouth hardened. 'She was pregnant with Vincente's child when she arrived in Britain but disappeared shortly after it was born. Father never found her. She's been missing for over twenty-five years.'

Something knotted in Ginny's stomach. And the penny dropped. 'You said your father had taken care of her!' she accused shakily.

'He did for a little while. And then she vanished.'

Her breathing became shallow. Of course. Vincente wouldn't have been searching for his daughter...unless he'd known that his wife was pregnant before she left. Although Mary had disappeared, Vincente had finally traced his wife to the nursing home. And he'd placed that advert because Ginny's date and place of birth were right—even if her mother had called herself Sarah Temple.

Vincente's wife and her mother could well be one and the same person. And that meant that Vincente might be her father. She remembered Pascal's fair hair. The colour drained from her face.

'Your aunt Mary's child would be twenty-five years old now, wouldn't she? I'm twenty-five, Leo,' she said in a low voice.

Leo's glacial eyes flicked briefly to hers. 'Yes,' he replied softly.

CHAPTER SEVEN

GINNY let out a little whimper. Leo's hand reached out to cover hers while she sat there, numb with shock. She almost wished that she hadn't made the link. Mary had been pregnant. Disturbed. Ginny shuddered. Her mother had been disturbed too. Suddenly she wanted to deny any connection with both Mary and Vincente. She lifted tearful eyes to Leo's.

'I should have listened to you,' she said shakily. 'I should have left well alone.'

'I'm sorry,' he said, sounding a little stilted. 'I did my best not to wash my family's dirty linen in public but you were determined to find out why I was being evasive, weren't you?'

No sympathy. Only an accusation. Peevishly she drew her hand away. 'So what's the story?' she said dully.

'You already know that Mary was pregnant when she left Vincente,' he muttered. 'When Father got her back to England she was thirty years old, in shock from the journey and naturally disturbed. For a while she stayed secretly in Castlestowe. Father and she decided to hide her condition even from Grandfather. It was the perfect place to hide because it was winter and the castle would be shut up till the season began.'

Ginny nodded. She knew what he meant by that. The social circuit had a set plan and the earl only used the castle from May to September. Amid thousands of acres of gorse and grouse moors, it would have been the perfect place to hide.

'It must have been like a morgue up there,' she said quietly. She looked out at the street below, oranges, reds and yellows predominating in the sunshine. And she thought of grey, unwelcoming Castlestowe. 'A cold, wet, bleak change after St Lucia. Poor woman. What a culture shock. But...you said she disappeared from Castlestowe. What links her with the Glasgow nursing home?'

'The records,' explained Leo. 'Father told me that she was definitely there. I imagine Vincente had Mary traced there too. His investigators would have followed up all the women with children born around the right time and eliminated them in turn. So I presume they were left with a handful of untraceable mothers who might fit the picture. You were obviously born in the right nursing home on the right day.'

She sat there as still as stone and let that sink in. The truth had been kept from her by Leo because she might be his cousin and he wouldn't want her to be part of his family—especially now that they were divorced. It would be too awkward to admit that the notorious model was part of the Brandon line. Everyone knew that she wasn't good enough.

'Your aunt—what did she look like?' she asked shakily.

'Grandfather got rid of all the photographs. Father was too cut up to talk about her much.'

He sounded angry. Hostile. Despair robbed her body of all its strength. Leo loathed Vincente. And she could be Vincente's daughter. A soft shudder ran through her body and Leo silently handed her his glass, in which an inch or two of rum remained.

'Thanks,' she mumbled, and tossed it back. It revived her brain a little. 'How long have you known?' she asked in a hoarse croak.

'Since I mentioned to Father that you'd gone to St Lucia in search of St Honoré. He was appalled and told me then.'

Ginny wanted to cry. But they were in public and she didn't cry in front of strangers. It was probably the reason why Leo had insisted that they talk here. He knew that she'd rather bottle up her tears and her anger than expose her emotions to others.

'You have no idea where your aunt is?' she whispered miserably.

'None. She could be anywhere. She could be dead.'

'I have to find out!' she said jerkily. 'More so now than before! It all fits, doesn't it? My mother being poor and friendless, the fact that she'd been traumatised by something—it might have been because of everything she'd suffered at Vincente's hands. It would explain why she couldn't bring herself to touch me, why she hated me, why she developed a phobia, why she gave me away—'

'Ginny,' he growled, 'calm down and think now. There are some serious consequences of this situation, the first being Vincente—'

'He's a *monster*!' she said angrily.

Leo gave a curt nod. 'Thank God you realise that now. I want you to promise me you won't try to see him—'

'But I have to!' she cried vehemently. 'Don't you see that? Unless I do, I'll never know! He'll describe my mother. There might be photographs that'll jog my memory. Something to tell us for sure either way. I must find out the truth, Leo. I have to learn it from him.'

She bit her lip to stop the self-pitying tears from spilling out. No time for tears. It was imperative that she go to Beau Rivage and confront Vincente.

'Hell!' Leo removed his hand from hers and ran it through his silky brown hair in weary exasperation. 'Have you thought this through? You go to Vincente, he seems convinced, you take the DNA tests. Then what? What exactly will you do if you *are* his daughter? Live happily ever after with him? What's the *point*, Ginny?' he snapped irritably.

Feeling very alone and vulnerable, Ginny stared miserably at him, the rest of her life suddenly a terrifying prospect. Her soft mouth trembled.

'I don't know,' she admitted. 'I only know that I've been someone else for so long—playing the part of a successful international model—that I don't know who I really am any more. When I first came here, I hoped to find out. I wish I'd never meddled, but I have.' Angrily she scooped up a wilful tear with her fingertip. 'So I've got to go ahead, haven't I? Because I know I'll never settle to anything till I've uncovered the real truth about my background. And all I can do is take one step at a time.'

'It might be a coincidence that you were born in the home,' Leo pointed out. 'You can't have been the only baby to arrive that day.'

'No,' she acknowledged. 'The solicitor I spoke to said there'd been another woman who'd come here in response to Vincente's advert. Since the solicitor had heard nothing from her, he'd assumed she wasn't Vincente's daughter. Now it's for me to learn the truth.'

'I warn you,' he said softly, his eyes boring into hers, 'if Vincente should ever learn you've been married to me, he'd say you were his daughter even if you weren't, just for spite. He's that kind of man. Don't imagine you'll necessarily get the truth from him.'

'I didn't get it from you, did I?' she whispered miserably.

Leo's eyes kindled. 'There was a reason for my evasiveness, Ginny. Protection—'

'Yes,' she said impatiently. 'Of the Brandon name. But my peace of mind is more important to me.'

She hesitated, knowing what she wanted to say but scared that she might be turned down. Nausea gripped her stomach. Facing Vincente alone would be a horrific ordeal. She could only do it with Leo. Nervously she shifted in her seat and fiddled with the cutlery.

'I haven't completely absorbed all this. But...it's going to be hard to cope with.' Her eyes lifted in appeal. His face was blank. She'd have to crawl, then. 'Leo, if I've never asked you for a favour before, I'm asking now,' she said, trying to keep the panic out of her voice. 'I— I am going to see Vincente. And I can't do it alone. Please!' she begged, her huge eyes moist with unshed tears. 'We don't have to say who you are, but...I want you to come with me...'

'So I'm useful to you now?' he asked.

Ginny flushed. 'You're making this difficult for me,' she said quietly. 'It would suit you to come, after all! You can be Leo McKenzie if you like—but I think it might be better if you were with me, don't you?'

'For the last time, I'm asking you to forget this. If you're hoping that Vincente will make you rich and get you out of debt, I'll give you money. I'll pay your court fees—'

'I've almost done that,' she snapped, her tattered nerves driving her almost to screaming point. 'This is personal. Can't you see that I have to know? If you'll come with me, I'll do anything you want, Leo,' she promised rashly.

He leaned back nonchalantly in his chair, his gaze slowly raking her tense body. 'Anything?' There was a brutally long silence while he held her a prisoner of his charcoal-dark eyes. Tingles of fear sped through her as a gleam appeared in them—a gleam that became a mocking light. 'That's a promise I can't refuse. So yes, I'll go with you to see Vincente,' he drawled. 'Between us, we'll find out whether he's your father or not—and I'll help you to find your mother. That I swear on the honour of the Brandons.'

'And...' Her tongue slipped nervously along her dry lips. 'The price?' she asked huskily.

He smiled and she knew with a sinking heart that the cat had the cream again. What would he demand? Unlimited sex? Never to see her again? Her guaranteed silence if Vincente was her father, never revealing that she'd once been a Brandon? Her unhappy eyes pleaded with his, waiting for his answer.

Leo leaned forward till his mouth was a few inches from hers. 'I'll tell you the price when you know for certain if you're his daughter or not.'

'That makes a difference?' she asked, dry-mouthed.

Swiftly he kissed her, his mouth moistening hers. Miserable and confused, she lifted her hands to his face and held him while she returned the kiss with all her heart. When the pressure of his mouth had gone, she opened her drowsy eyes, her lashes fluttering with the shudders of tension that contact with him always produced.

'The bargain is sealed, Ginny,' he said softly. 'And yes, knowing who you are makes a difference.' He stood up. 'We'll go now. Ready?'

Something held her to the chair—a premonition that Leo would destroy her if she was Vincente's daughter. But there was only one way to find out. 'Yes,' she said hoarsely. 'I'm ready.'

'Beau Rivage?' Joseph turned the launch south out of Castries then looked curiously at Leo. 'You got someone meeting you on the beach?'

'No, we haven't,' replied Leo with a faint frown. 'Why?'

Ginny clutched his arm anxiously. They'd decided to give Vincente no warning—and, if he wasn't at home, to wait there till near dark in the hope he'd return. There would be servants around, surely? 'Is that a problem?' she asked.

'Long, long walk,' said Joseph. 'Track's probably overgrown. The master of Beau Rivage don't get out much and he don't look after the plantation.'

'Should we go back to the hotel and take a taxi?' suggested Leo.

'No way!' laughed Joseph. 'Not unless you like riding the road from hell! Tell you something, man—I can set you down at Beau Jardin. That's the next bay. Someone there can run you over to Rivage by truck. They might not go all the way, but they'll get you close enough. OK?'

'Thanks, Joseph. We'd appreciate that,' Leo smiled and steadied Ginny against the sway of the boat as they made their way to the seats in the stern.

It was nice having his arm briefly around her waist but he withdrew it all too soon. Surreptitiously she wriggled closer to him, wanting the comfort of his body because she felt sick with nerves. 'My hands are shaking. This is worse than appearing in a big show,' she said ruefully.

'You'll be all right.' Leo slid an arm around her shoulders. 'I'm with you, aren't I?' he said drily.

'My hero!' she joked, but felt as if that was true.

They both fell silent. Ginny spent the journey preparing herself mentally and emotionally for the meeting. Vincente would be some kind of sick and embittered old man, an ogre, and she'd hate him on sight. But she had to remain polite otherwise he'd never tell her anything. Somehow she had to gain his confidence—and since everyone obviously found him impossible that would be a tall order.

'You're very pale. And very cold.' Leo rubbed warmth into her body. 'It won't take long,' he said huskily. 'Then it'll be over with.'

Ginny gazed at him helplessly and found herself torn in two. It would be a relief to have it all over. But then would come the payment that Leo intended to demand. And then, probably, she'd never see him again.

'Beau Jardin!' came Joseph's shout after a while.

Startled, Ginny looked towards the coastline ahead, her heart pounding with apprehension. However, Beau Jardin looked so beautiful and serene that she felt herself relax a little.

'It's lovely!' she said softly.

'Civilisation, thank God! I was afraid it might be as deserted as Rivage. Looks like we will be able to find someone to drive us over for sure,' commented Leo, indicating the collection of assorted boats in the glassy bay.

The launch slowed and began to motor between the anchored yachts, launches and pirogues, the brightly painted dugouts used as water taxis. They approached the desert island beach—gently lapping waves, pale honey sand, coconut palms dipping to the water. And, set on the cliff that protected the almost landlocked bay, Ginny saw a white stone house with green jalousies and a blaze of colourful gardens around it.

'Gorgeous house,' she said.

'Splendid,' he agreed. 'Whoever lives here is worth a bob or two. Busy place, isn't it?'

There seemed to be a number of families swimming and chatting on the beach and she wondered if this was another secluded hotel. She looked towards Joseph to ask, but he was concentrating hard, his face screwed up with effort.

'I can hear music,' she cried in surprise.

Joseph had been manoeuvring the launch to the jetty and the roar of the reversing engines had masked the sound. Now she could clearly hear a steel band—and saw it too, under the shade of the palms.

'I think we've gatecrashed a party!' Leo frowned.

They were people of all shapes and sizes—an old St Lucian couple or two sitting in the shade of a gazebo, a horde of children splashing happily in the water, people in bathing costumes, casual T-shirts and shorts, elegant tropical suits and floaty dresses.

'It looks fun,' she said wistfully, clambering onto the wooden jetty. 'Thanks, Joseph! Bye, everyone!' She managed a smile and a wave as the boat motored away with its quota of hotel guests bound for Castries. 'I'm so nervous,' she confided shakily to Leo.

'Take my hand,' he said gruffly. 'We'll find the host or hostess and arrange transport.'

Ginny groaned in dismay. 'No need,' she said, aghast. 'I think she's found us! Oh, Leo! This is too much!'

'Good Lord!' he exclaimed. 'Isn't that the woman...?'

Gulping, Ginny nodded. Coming towards them was the brunette who'd burst into Ginny's room, rasped Pascal's name in distress and then fainted. Stunned, she watched the woman approach, taking in the mass of shining brown hair, the simple white string-strap dress, the sweet face tense with anxiety.

'Pascal's wife!' she whispered in horror, and her cheeks flared scarlet with embarrassment at the confrontation.

'I'll protect you,' Leo said under his breath. 'I won't let anyone hurt you.' His eyes slanted to hers when she raised a bewildered face. 'You represent an investment,' he drawled cynically. 'One I mean to share.'

Her mind whirled. Everyone wanted a piece of her. Agents, publicists, managers and now Leo—presumably because she might stand to gain from Vincente's estate! She was only a commodity to them. Not a person at all. 'You want to own a share in Ginny McKenzie?' she asked bitterly.

'Absolutely,' he replied, smoothly suave. 'So let me defend you if necessary. We'll present a united front and I'll inflate my chest a bit. Always impressive.'

'Does nothing for me,' she muttered crossly.

'Smile, sweetheart. Or put on that Grace Kelly stare that freezes blood. Good afternoon, Mrs St Honoré,' he said politely.

The woman had eyes only for the mortified Ginny. 'Good afternoon,' she said in a quietly modulated voice.

'Can I help you?' she asked warily, faint disdain on her generous mouth.

'I hope so.' Ginny took her cue from Pascal's wife and adopted a polite, distant manner. 'We were wondering if...' She licked her lips. The woman was so hostile and Ginny cringed with shame.

'Can anyone here give us a lift into Beau Rivage?' Leo asked commandingly. And for once Ginny blessed his air of authority.

The woman drew in a sharp breath. 'No,' she said flatly. 'Walk. It's about three miles. If you find the right track. Watch out for the snakes.'

Ginny glanced up at Leo. He'd gone white. The only thing he feared. And she knew that the deadly fer-de-lance inhabited the rainforest together with boa constrictors which had been brought to the island ages ago to keep the slaves on the sugar plantations.

'I know why you're being unhelpful. But I think you've misjudged my wife,' Leo said tightly. 'She—'

'Your *wife*?' Obviously surprised, the woman directed her large hazel eyes at Leo and then smiled the kind of smile at them both that melted hearts. 'Oh, I'm so glad! It *was* a mistake! Thank goodness!'

Ginny let out a sigh of relief. This wouldn't be so hard as she'd imagined. 'Mrs St Honoré—'

'Mandy, please,' she said encouragingly.

'Mandy.' Ginny hesitantly returned the beaming smile. 'I'm Ginny McKenzie. This is Leo. Look...I know how it must have seemed to you,' she said, her face hot and burning with the memory, 'but I'd been taking a shower and your husband came in and—'

'Oh, *that*!' dismissed Mandy, as if finding her husband glued to a half-dressed woman were a mere trifle. 'Please don't worry about that. Pascal explained. He'll be mortified that he was so curt with you. You must have been poleaxed! No, something else was bothering me. We thought you... No. It doesn't matter. It's all right now, though,' she said contentedly.

Leo's hand tightened around Ginny's waist and she remembered that he'd said that Pascal would not welcome a sister who'd share Vincente's legacy. 'I think we deserve an explanation. What *were* you worried about?' he asked softly.

It was Mandy's turn to look embarrassed. 'It really isn't important now,' she said awkwardly.

'Surely we have a right to know?' insisted Leo gravely.

Mandy sighed. 'All right. It's not exactly the greatest kept secret in the world. Pascal thought...' She shuffled her feet awkwardly then looked at Ginny. 'He was certain you'd come to St Lucia to be Vincente's mistress!' she said wryly.

'I *beg* your pardon?' gasped Ginny, deeply offended.

'What?' cried Leo.

'He had good reason—honestly,' explained Mandy. 'Vincente had recently advertised for a companion/ housekeeper. When Pascal heard you'd been asking for his father, he thought—' Ginny gasped and Mandy gave her an understanding look. 'I know; it's awful, isn't it? But everyone here is aware that he likes young women around him to fetch and carry for him. To read to him and keep him company. And... and so on,' she finished delicately, blushing beneath her tan.

'Not surprising the man's sick,' muttered Leo viciously.

Ginny winced, praying fervently that Vincente wasn't her father. She was getting cold feet. Maybe she wouldn't go to Rivage.

Mandy sighed. 'Pascal thinks it's a kind of macho thing with him. Every now and then women float in—usually from England—and Vincente gives them the once-over. Sometimes he employs them, though they never stay long. It's no wonder that the hotel is suspicious of any beautiful woman asking for Vincente St Honoré.'

'They. . .' Ginny gulped. 'They thought I was a candidate too? Leo,' she said faintly, 'that's why no one would tell me where he lived!'

'Or maybe Pascal asked them not to.' Leo's dark eyes bored into Mandy and she dropped guilty eyes. 'I thought so.'

'None of us have wanted to be associated with what Vincente does,' said Mandy quietly. 'People would rather he didn't live on the island. Everyone shuns him, other than the few who work for him. Please, Ginny, forgive us for misunderstanding, but you can see why Pascal was so angry. He was fed up with Vincente's companions being dumped when he was bored with them and fed up with them demanding their air fare home and weeping on his shoulder.'

'Is Pascal here?' asked Leo curtly. 'I want to talk to him.'

'Of course.' Mandy led them back along the jetty. 'What a shock you must have had when Pascal burst in on you and then I did a dying-swan act on your quarry tiles!' Mandy giggled and Ginny found herself smiling back. 'We'll find Pascal and he can apologise and explain. I'm so glad you came, Ginny. Pascal tried to reach you this morning to invite you to lunch.' She grinned. 'He wanted to stop you meeting his father.'

Ginny shuddered delicately. 'He would have been doing me a favour,' she muttered.

'So...' Mandy's big hazel eyes slanted up to Ginny's '...why ever would you want to see such a horrible man?' she asked frankly.

'I think we'd like to discuss that with Pascal,' said Leo coolly, pressing warning fingers into Ginny's shoulder.

'All right.' Mandy didn't seem offended at all. 'Well,' she said cheerfully, 'I hope you'll stay here for a while. We're having such fun. Lunch is over, but it looks like the party's going on till midnight, because we'll be dancing on the beach. Oh, and we're serving tea soon. Chocolate cake with chocolate butter-cream included, by my request!' Her delighted laughter tinkled out. 'I can ask for almost anything now I'm pregnant,' she grinned.

'Oh! Congratulations,' said Ginny warmly.

Mandy flung an arm out to embrace the beach, the dense foliage in the valley and the house on the cliff. 'It's wonderful, isn't it? Welcome to Beau Jardin. Welcome to our home,' she said softly.

'Thank you,' Ginny said, responding to Mandy's frank, open nature.

'Pascal's making sandcastles,' chattered Mandy, leading them from the jetty along the beach, and Ginny tried to imagine the flaxen-haired dynamo doing anything that ordinary. 'Practising to be a father,' she said gently, her expression like that of a Madonna.

And Ginny felt a twist of envy. This woman was deeply happy, with a loving husband and a child growing in her body. She felt herself trembling, and acknowledged with a grateful look the pressure of Leo's hand on her waist.

When Mandy turned to speak to a small child and exclaim over a collection of hibiscus petals, Leo whispered, 'Whatever you do, don't tell Pascal or Mandy why we're here. Or that you might be Vincente's daughter. Accept Pascal's apologies and any invitation to stay for the afternoon. I can see some four-wheel drives up at the house. I'll find someone on his staff who'll run us over.'

Ginny nodded and then smiled as Mandy turned back to them and they continued on across the beach, smiling and waving at people as they went.

'You're not the only one Pascal accused of applying for the job of Vincente's mistress,' Mandy confided to Ginny. 'I'd answered an advert, you see, and Pascal thought it was one of Vincente's—you know the kind. Housekeeper/companion required for rich man of property, fiftyish, quiet location, send photograph and measurements. View to marriage.' Mandy smiled ruefully. 'The marriage bit was just the bait. Vincente's been catching women with it for years.'

'An . . . advert?' said Ginny faintly. She and Leo exchanged puzzled looks.

'Yes.' She gave Ginny a curious look—one that Ginny knew only too well. 'Don't I know you from somewhere—other than your hotel room? I didn't get much of a look at you last time—my mind was on other things,' she said ruefully. 'But I *have* seen you before, haven't I?'

Ginny consciously stopped walking from the hips and leading with her shoulders. 'I've no idea,' she said evasively. 'Is that your husband there?' she asked.

'Hi, darling!' yelled Mandy. 'Look who I've found!'

Leo's hand tightened around Ginny's when the tanned, muscular figure rose and dusted the sand from his shins and hands, his searing blue eyes fixed on the pale-faced Ginny. Mandy made the introductions, related their conversation to Pascal and tactfully excused herself.

'I was going to apologise to you even if you *were* applying for the job as Vincente's companion,' Pascal said quietly. 'Mind you, I would have warned you off. Now it's obvious you're not, I can only say I hope you'll forgive me for my behaviour. I was way out of line and I hope you'll accept our hospitality and spend the rest of the day here. Perhaps you would stay the night?'

'Oh, we couldn't—' began Ginny uncomfortably.

'That's very generous,' broke in Leo with unusual geniality. 'We'd be delighted. Thanks. And we'd very much like to join in your party. Is it for any special celebration?'

Pascal smiled. 'Just a get-together of our friends. I like to see my wife enjoying herself, Mr McKenzie. I'll arrange for a room to be prepared for you. We can lend you whatever you need. In the meantime, feel free to wander around. Mandy and I will catch up with you later. Excuse me.'

Ginny waited till he'd gone before she rounded on Leo. 'Why did you do that?' she asked angrily. 'We'll be put in a room together! I don't want that; you don't either! And what about Beau Rivage?'

'Look at the time, Ginny,' he said softly. 'It's getting late. I'd already been worrying that by the time we got ourselves to Rivage it would be dusk. We'd have to spend the night *there*. I don't think that's a good idea. If we stay here tonight, we can leave early in the morning. We'll be more likely to catch Vincente at home.'

It made sense. But Ginny couldn't help wondering if Leo was pulling her strings again. Her eyes chilled. She wouldn't dance like an obedient puppet for him! 'I hope you're good at sleeping on floors,' she said crossly, and walked off.

By the evening, however, her irritability and suspicions had faded into the background. Everyone was so friendly, and she'd found herself chatting away to people with more ease than she'd ever known. It was the first party she'd ever been to whilst wearing casual clothes and comfortable loafers—and the first where she hadn't needed to remember that she was on show.

She met Pascal's aunt Susannah, who looked young enough to be his older sister with her curly blonde hair and youthful face. Ginny smiled to see the obvious deep love between them as they teased one another unmercifully.

And then Ginny stripped off her shirt and helped the delightful Mandy to build sand boats for the children, occasionally glancing up to watch Leo obligingly curling up to provide a vaulting horse for them. She ached to her very bones as their eyes met in a paralysing moment when they were both surrounded by laughing children.

The soft affection on Leo's face drew a low groan from her lips. And she knew she must look as wistful as he did. They could have been playing with their own children by now. They'd both wasted an opportunity. Wasted love. What fools, she thought bitterly.

Darkness fell early, as it always did in the Tropics. Many people stayed for the barbecue on the beach. Ginny sat on the sand waiting for the food to be cooked, staring at the glinting silver path made by the bright moonlight on the black sea.

'Crayfish gumbo, snapper and buttered salmon. OK?'
Leo dropped down beside her and handed her one of
the two plates he'd brought. He looked at her as she
silently picked at the food. 'Don't you like it?' he asked
quietly.

'Yes.' Her fork speared a plump piece of salmon and
she lifted it to her mouth where it virtually melted. 'It's
wonderful. Everything's wonderful,' she sighed. Her
head tipped back and she scanned the hugeness of the
midnight darkness above where the stars seemed to
twinkle with a sharper brilliance than she'd ever known.
Palm-fronds waved overhead in the faint evening breeze,
silhouetted black against the sequinned backdrop of the
sky.

'I know I'm on edge, and there are various aspects of
this situation I don't care for,' she said thoughtfully, 'but
I've enjoyed myself more this afternoon than I have
for...oh, as long as I can remember. And I find that
vaguely confusing,' she admitted.

Leo rested a hand on the nape of her neck, his fingers
lightly massaging her sensitive skin there. 'I've enjoyed
it too,' he said huskily. 'Mandy is one of the nicest
women I've ever met. Pascal, for all his natural suspicions about us, is the kind of man I'd like as a friend.
This is the kind of place I could make my home,' he
said surprisingly. 'How about you?'

'Yes,' she found herself saying, so surprised was she
by his admission. He loved Castlestowe. He was its heir.
It was the holiday mood talking. But she really felt a
kinship with this particular part of St Lucia—something
deeper than a romantic sentimentality. 'I'd like that,'
she whispered, her eyes dreamy.

Dreams, she thought sadly. Nothing but dreams. Of sitting on a beach of their own, with Leo, listening to the sounds of the jungle, wandering up to their house...

'I envy Pascal and Mandy,' murmured Leo. His voice sounded thicker. 'They've left the rat race. No pretending. No duty. No relentless drive to achieve. They're working with nature and yet they have glamour and romance in their lives too. And friends—good friends—who'll be there when they're needed.'

'You couldn't give up Castlestowe,' she said flatly.

The caressing fingers stilled. 'Let's forget everything we *should* be doing and carry on dreaming, shall we?' he said lightly.

And because she wanted to be in his arms on this beautiful night she put down her plate and took his hand. They walked through the densely planted palms along a path lit by low flares stuck in the sand. Her heart felt as if it would burst with the romance of the night. Ahead, in a small clearing beyond the pretty gazebo—where she was sure she'd seen Pascal and Mandy wrapped in a clinch—she could see softly coloured lights strung from the branches of almond trees.

And musicians sat on upturned oil-drums, their faces smiling above their violins and shakers as they played a haunting, lilting tune that stole behind Ginny's defences and fatally weakened her limbs.

Without a word, Leo held out his arms and she drifted into them. They were so good together, moving as if they needed no conscious thought to follow each other's steps.

Ginny sighed and rested her cheek against Leo's. His mouth touched her ear. Nibbled. Sent delicious tremors

through her body. Of course she couldn't allow that.
She'd stop him. Soon.

But it felt like a dream and she was unwilling to wake
up. He began to cradle her body closer, his hand sliding
up her spine under the brief cropped top. The touch of
his lips on her ear, his warm breath, the exciting male
power in every tense muscle—all combined to drive her
deeper into a state of suspense.

Why should she deny herself pleasure? she argued.
Soon he'd be gone. Married to his suitable woman. Pride
struggled with desire. If he genuinely wanted her, and
wasn't going to treat her with contempt afterwards, she
wouldn't be able to refuse him. Maybe that was stupid.
But it was honest. The only problem was being sure that
he was sincere. Her instincts weren't too good where he
was concerned.

'Ginny?'

'Mmm?'

'Ginny!' he sighed in her ear. 'Oh, God! Ginny!'

His mouth crushed hers, fierce and demanding. And
she responded without hesitation, groaning as he coaxed
her lips apart in the quiet privacy of the darkness where
he had taken her. 'Leo!' she whispered helplessly.

'I want you. I've wanted you all afternoon. All
morning. I'm going crazy, Ginny!' he growled, savagely
kissing her long, slender throat. 'You're so beautiful!
Your skin is so smooth and it smells so good. I want to
kiss every part of your body. I want to hold you and
make love to you and I want us to pretend that nothing
else exists, that we're on a desert island and there are no
problems, no difficulties between us, only the night, a
bed, and you and me. Can we do that, Ginny?' he asked

passionately, his eyes glittering with a smouldering sensuality.

'No reproaches, no recriminations?' she husked shakily.

He shook his head, his hand on his heart. And then he drew her hand there so that she could feel the violence of the heavy beat beneath his ribs. In a gesture that made her own heart turn over, he kissed her hand intently, his eyes never leaving hers. And silently they walked up to the house, to their room with the breathtaking view of the sea far below.

Leo flung open all the floor-to-ceiling jalousies and lit candles in the room. 'Take your clothes off for me,' he said softly. 'I want to watch you.'

Without any shame, she undressed for him, knowing that he found her body beautiful tonight. The light played on her skin, flattering it by casting a soft golden light that emphasised the curves of her breasts and buttocks and the glint of white-blonde hair in the inviting triangle above her gleaming thighs.

'And you,' she whispered, her voice almost robbed of its power.

'You undress me,' he said huskily.

Ginny found herself undulating towards him, every inch of her body engaged in his seduction. 'It could take some time,' she said teasingly.

He licked his lips. 'Take however long you need,' he growled.

But she saw that he had clenched his teeth together as if he needed to control himself. And she smiled, slowly easing out each button of his shirt, her fingers drifting wonderingly over the hot wall of his chest as she did so.

Then she bent to unlace his casual shoes. Leo groaned and drew her up again, lifting her in his arms and carrying her to the bed. Joy filled her heart. She loved him so much that it hurt her with a deep, piercing pain. She almost blurted out her feelings. Almost. Something stopped her, even in the wildness of their lovemaking. Because she had to survive afterwards, when she was alone. And if she gave her heart to Leo again she'd never be able to get it back.

So in the explosions of emotion in her mind, the passionate climaxes of her body she knew a bitterness so tangible that she could feel it building up inside her, till it overflowed in a torrent of sobbing that not even all her self-discipline could control.

'No tears,' he murmured. 'No tears, sweetheart.'

She winced at the endearment and wept into the pillow while he stroked her hair and removed wet strands from her hot face.

'We've made a mess of things,' she sniffed.

'We're both strong, independent people. Neither of us is used to making compromises. I think we're ready to make concessions to one another now, aren't we?'

'What kind of concessions?' she asked cautiously. Her heart thudded like a wild thing and she tried not to read too much into Leo's words.

'In our lifestyles,' he answered quietly. 'We have to find some way of living together. I don't want to be apart from you any longer.'

She studied his face, holding back her overwhelming delight. There was no future in living with Leo as his mistress. 'I could never trust you,' she said flatly, wishing that it were not so painfully true.

'Because of Arabella?' He kissed her sulky mouth and turned her face so that she was forced to look into his eyes. 'I didn't make love to her.'

'I heard you both. I saw you in bed with her,' she reminded him jerkily.

'You were meant to.' He smiled wryly at her gasp. 'It was the only thing I could think of to get you out of my hair.'

'Why should you want to?' she asked indignantly.

'I couldn't bear to have you near me, knowing that other men had touched you,' he told her gently. 'I believed you'd been unfaithful and it was tearing me apart, destroying me, inch by inch.'

'You're the only man who's ever made love to me,' she said quietly. 'I couldn't...I could never have given myself to anyone else. Sex is such a private, intimate part of my life.' She blushed. 'You know how long it took you to make any headway with me. You remember how difficult it was for me to let you touch me on our wedding night. Whatever my public face suggests about my sophistication, you and I know that I find it hard to reveal myself to anyone—let alone a chance male for a one-night stand.'

Leo let out a long sigh. 'I know that now,' he admitted. 'But we'd become so distant that I felt I didn't know you any more. In my fevered mind anything was possible.'

'So...what happened with Arabella?' she asked hesitantly.

'I asked her to pretend to fool around in bed with me because I thought that was the only way I could persuade you to walk out on me. And she was more than willing. It went no further than what you saw. I swear it. I just want to put the record straight. Do you believe me?' he finished anxiously.

Ginny closed her eyes in despair. The accusations about her in the press had destroyed her marriage—and if they'd stopped to talk things through instead of reacting in anger she and Leo could have saved it.

'I believe you,' she said, her voice full of regret.

He gave her one of his slow, warming smiles. 'That's all I want to hear. We'll see Vincente in the morning. One of the banana-packers seemed sure that he was at home. And after that...'

Ginny froze, all tears suspended. 'After that, what?'

'You owe me, remember?' he said softly, kissing a tear that was trickling perilously towards the end of her nose.

'I—owe—you!' she repeated. 'What...what do you want from me?' She wanted to add that he had everything already, that she had nothing more to give.

'Marriage,' he replied, suddenly serious. 'I want us to get married again.'

CHAPTER EIGHT

IT WAS everything Ginny had longed for. She was more than ready to make changes in her life and approach marriage with different values—but what about Leo? Would he really be prepared to make concessions and sacrifices?

'Why?' she asked shakily.

'This, my darling.'

She felt his mouth surround her nipple and closed her eyes, yielding helplessly to the gentle devastation. 'It's not enough for marriage,' she rasped. 'And what about...?' Her groan was stopped by his kiss, long and coaxing, and the slide of her body against his made her want to sigh in despair. Angrily she pushed him back, fixed him with blazing tawny eyes and said jerkily, 'What...about...Miss Suitable?'

'Who?' he murmured in amusement, his beautiful head lowering as he began to graze her shoulder with his teeth. And the soft flesh at her waist, her hip...

'Is...?' Ginny moaned, fighting off his marauding hands. They were going too far, too fast; she wasn't ready—well, she was, but she would not go any further till she knew why he should have changed his mind so dramatically and...

He was kissing her mind away. A great surge of love overwhelmed her, blasting any sense into a million pieces that she'd never put together while he held her like this, touched her with such delicacy. Pressure. Just enough, perfect, so attuned to her body that he knew how to spin her into that mindless world of total pleasure. And she was spinning, everything forgotten again as she sought to be the most seductive, the most alluring woman he'd ever set eyes on.

I love you, she said silently as his eyes adored her body, arching voluptuously to him. I love you, she thought with deeper passion as he groaned and kissed the entire surface of her skin while she stretched and writhed in bliss and frustration.

'I love you,' she whispered somewhere in the darkness of the soft night. Maybe she'd said it aloud. She didn't know. There was a blur between fantasy and reality. 'I love you. I love you.'

She would give anything to be with this man for the rest of her life. Even her pride. A shiver ran through her as his dark form hovered over her, his eyes suddenly blazing with a feral brilliance. And her hand reached up to caress his face at the same time as his reached out to stroke hers. Perhaps she was being a fool...

'Ginny!' husked his teasing voice. 'You're frowning!'

Her wandering finger traced his aristocratic nose, the well-bred mouth that echoed the mouths of his ancestors, a relic of eight hundred years of power and authority. It smiled and nibbled her finger, shaping into sultry lines. For her. But...

'How can I trust you?' she whispered, her eyes huge with anxiety.

He smiled in a loving way that made her heart lurch. 'Because I am trustworthy and because you have to. Let's talk in the morning. I want you, *now*, tonight.'

And he smiled his bemused, knee-weakening smile, his eyes so warm and worshipping that she found her tense muscles slowly relaxing, her flesh seeming to melt into a liquid that flowed into him. This was real love, she thought when a million stars burst in her heart as he kissed her with a poignant tenderness. And then she surrendered herself totally and could think no more.

The sky glowed with dawn embers when she floated back from the turbulent hours spent in Leo's arms. Gradually collecting her drifting thoughts, she lay supine against the bulk of his sleeping body, wondering what was so different about his lovemaking.

Something more desperate and fierce had marked his demands. An exciting, ruthless determination. But there had been so much gentleness, a touching restraint sometimes, as if his greatest wish had been to please her. And she'd been the one who hadn't been able to wait, who'd encouraged him to release his hunger and take his passion to the limits.

Ginny cautiously stretched her body. It felt loved. She smiled dreamily. Leo had been like a real lover. So attentive that if she didn't know better she could have sworn...

Her heart flipped in shock. Everything he'd done, the way he'd looked at her, the way he'd touched her with wonder and awe—every gesture and word had told her that he loved her. If so, the marriage would work, because they'd make sure it did this time. But—

'Marry me,' came his velvet voice, drowsy with sleep. He rolled over and grinned his heart-stopping grin.

Unfair, so early in the morning, she thought ruefully. She felt weak and drained of all energy to defy him— or to deny herself. He'd smashed all her defences and she hadn't time to put them up again. 'I'd be mad to,' she mumbled, watching the paddle fan turning, round and round.

'Marry me,' he coaxed with infinite seductiveness.

And his body was so warm and he held her so lovingly that she knew it would be impossible to refuse him whatever he wanted. 'We'd have to solve the problem of my work—'

'And Castlestowe,' he said, pre-empting her. 'I know. We can do that if we both really want to make our relationship work. I do. I think you want to as well. I know it'll take you a little while to be convinced—but you do want to marry me, don't you?'

How could she look into his eyes and deny that? 'Yes, I do,' she said shyly, and he hugged her. It would be all right, she told herself. This time it would be for ever.

Because they were both in such a happy mood, breakfast was very jolly. After Leo had made a business phone call to his father, they sat on the terrace overlooking the bay with Pascal and Mandy and Susannah, the sea a dazzling turquoise, the air perfumed with exuberant tropical flowers, the bird song almost overpowering.

And Ginny thought that there couldn't be a more perfect place on the island. Unfortunately, they had an unpleasant day ahead of them. Somehow Leo had to persuade Pascal to let him have transport to Beau Rivage. Breakfast was almost finished. They lingered over coffee, Pascal and Mandy holding hands—she and Leo too.

'I suppose you'll be wanting to get to Rivage,' said Pascal.

Susannah stiffened as if she'd been slapped and Ginny blinked in surprise. Before she could say anything, however, Leo had squeezed her hand in warning and was nodding at Pascal.

'I think we'd like to get it over with,' he said easily. He smiled at Ginny and kissed her frown-lines. 'Pascal and I had a chat during the party,' he explained. 'I explained we had business there.'

'What business?' asked Susannah harshly.

Ginny quailed under the piercing look that Susannah was giving her. Ginny wasn't happy with Leo's stretching of the truth. She liked Pascal and Mandy so much that she wanted them to be long-term friends. If they ever knew that she'd abused their hospitality, by omitting to tell them the true reason why she'd come to see Vincente, that friendship would founder. And Susannah looked ready to defend her beloved Pascal from anyone who might take a share of his inheritance.

'It's all right, Susannah,' said Pascal gently. 'Nothing to worry about.'

'That's what you think,' muttered his aunt, and left the table abruptly.

There was a surprised silence and then Pascal cleared his throat. 'There's a vehicle waiting outside for you. The keys will be in the ignition. Do you recall the way to Rivage from the map in my study?' he asked Leo.

'I do. Up to the flame-tree, turn right, keep going. Say *au revoir* to your aunt for me. See you later tonight, then.' Leo was embraced by Mandy and Pascal shook his hand.

'I don't envy you doing business with Vincente,' said Mandy wryly, hugging Ginny.

'Nor me.' Pascal bent his flax-blond head and kissed Ginny three times on her cheeks. 'Don't let him cheat you. Everything Vincente does is for himself. Remember that.'

They waved goodbye and drove off through the banana plantation and Ginny felt a great affection sweep over her. 'Pascal and I might be brother and sister,' she said reflectively, thinking that that must be the reason.

'Well . . . no.'

Ginny looked sharply at Leo. 'You sound worryingly certain about that! Did he say anything yesterday that's convinced you I'm nothing to do with Vincente?'

'On the contrary,' he replied softly. 'I'm almost certain you *are* his daughter. It's Pascal who's the odd one out. He's not Vincente's son, you see.'

Ginny gasped and Leo concentrated on steering for a moment while he negotiated a large pothole. 'For heaven's sake, Leo,' she said impatiently, 'you can't leave a remark like that hanging in the air! Explain what you mean!'

'Pascal and Vincente have always disliked one another. During a row, Vincente took much pleasure in telling Pascal that for the past thirty-two years he'd been hating the wrong father. So he has no claim to any inheritance.'

'Well, I'll be . . .' She twisted around as a thought suddenly struck her. 'Who told you?'

'One of Mandy's friends. Everyone knows, apparently.'

'Does his aunt know too?'

'Of course.'

'Then why was she so hostile when she knew where we were going? She'd been perfectly civil until then.'

'I don't know. Maybe she just hates Vincente. Yes, OK, I know it's not a convincing answer.' Leo thought for a moment. 'She's Vincente's younger sister, I gather.

Perhaps there's something else going on in that family that we don't know about. It's not important. Except for the fact that you might shortly be joining it.'

Her stomach knotted. 'You sound so sure,' she said tremulously. 'Why?'

'I rang my father before breakfast and talked to him. He admitted that he's convinced you're Mary's daughter. He said he had good reason to be so sure and that he could virtually guarantee it. Initially, he'd been hoping that you wouldn't insist on seeing Vincente. Since you were so determined, he said he had to confess that it's something he's suspected ever since he heard about your background. The same nursing home. The Glasgow connection. The way you look. Your age. Everything.'

'Oh, Leo!' she whispered.

'Father's conviction is good enough for me. Maybe that's why he hated the thought of us marrying. He loathes Vincente,' he muttered.

Ginny fell silent. Something she'd only been half believing had suddenly become very real. She was on her way to meet her father. How would she feel when she saw him? Repulsed? Disappointed? Ashamed?

Her lower lip wobbled annoyingly and she clenched her teeth. No use running scared now. She was in too deep. Shaking with nerves, she tried to compose herself.

They passed between neat rows of carefully tended bananas and occasional groups of fruit trees—mango, breadfruit, pawpaw, sour-sop, star apple... A garden of Eden, where everything flourished in the warm, damp soil.

And then, as if they were moving into a different world entirely, they passed the boundary-marking flame-tree and into a tangled wilderness.

'Vincente's land,' said Leo quietly. 'Pascal told me to warn you that it's reverted to nature. And that he lives in a shambles. Be prepared.' To her surprise, he reached over for her hand and kissed it. 'I'll be with you,' he said in a low tone. 'I'll make sure you come to no harm.'

'Thank you,' she said gratefully. 'Thank you.'

During the drive, seeing the neglect and the evidence of hurricane damage through the banana plantation, the occasional cocoa trees with the beans hanging black where they'd been eaten by tree rats, she became increasingly nervous, panic fluttering inside her breast like a terrified bird. When she finally caught sight of a building ahead, she reached out her hand to rest on Leo's shoulder for the reassurance of his strength and support.

'That must be the house,' she whispered nervously.

Once beautiful, it was now almost a ruin, the jalousies hanging off their hinges, the veranda roof leaning drunkenly and the wood of the single-storey house bleached white by the sun. There were traces of its former colonial grandeur—intricate carving on the posts and framework, evidence of a grand avenue of lofty king palms and ornamental flower-beds around an enormous lake thick with fabulous water lilies.

Ginny felt overcome with sadness.

'Wow!' exclaimed Leo in admiration, stopping to take in the still splendid sight. His eyes lifted to the dark green hills soaring into the sky—a magnificent backdrop for the ash-coloured house. 'This could be so beautiful!'

Ginny tensed. Either she was over-sensitive or there was something close to acquisitiveness in his tone. As if it was running through his mind that he might be master here one day. It would be justice, she thought, the idea coming to her out of the blue. And she quailed.

If he was married to her and she really was Vincente's daughter, Leo would jointly inherit Beau Rivage. Thus he would avenge his aunt. The Brandons would be appeased. Vincente had harmed one of his family—and the Brandons cared for their own, protected them against all others. Their motto, emblazoned on their silver and crockery and their notepaper, was 'Family First unto Death'. Ginny drew her trembling hand from Leo's shoulder. Was he marrying her purely to acquire Beau Rivage?

'Bear up,' he said softly, turning sparkling eyes on her. 'You'll be OK. Leave the talking to me.'

She couldn't have said anything if she'd tried. There was a huge lump in her throat and horror was churning up her stomach. Numb and blank with apprehension, she sat stiffly while Leo drove up to the veranda, and shakily stepped onto the weed-strewn drive.

Leo's arm came around her shoulders. She would have shrugged it away but she didn't think she could manage on her own. The front door was open and when no one answered their calls they went inside.

It was dark and smelt musty. Ginny gave an involuntary shiver. 'It's cold,' she whispered, looking up at the beautifully carved ceiling. And there was no joy in the house. Her glance took in the antiques, the carefully polished mahogany furniture, the delicate fruit woods, oriental vases, a French clock and matching mirror. Priceless rugs lay scattered on a floor the colour of honey and massive paintings in ornate gold frames crowded the panelled walls. Someone kept house for him. Someone cared for it, she thought.

'Hello!' called Leo into the silence.

'I suppose he's not at home,' she said, resigned to a wait. 'We could...' She paused. There had been a sound, deeper in the house. The sound of a man sobbing. The hairs prickled on the back of her neck. 'Leo!' she whispered, clutching him.

'I'll go—'

'No!' she squeaked. 'Don't leave me!'

'Damn! I should never have brought you! I should have come alone—'

'We have to see this through,' she said shakily. 'Together.'

The sound proved to be coming from behind a door at the end of the corridor. Leo tentatively turned the handle and pushed the door open while Ginny held her breath. A man with thinning grey hair was sitting on a comfortable chesterfield, weakly crying into a blue silk handkerchief.

Ginny felt her heart soften. This was no ogre. She firmly pushed Leo back, insisting with a jerk of her head that he didn't reveal himself. After a silent battle between them, he drew behind the door and she took a step into the room. 'Vincente,' she said gently.

He jumped, then turned and scowled, deep clefts gouged between his greying brows. 'Who the hell are you?' he demanded irritably.

'Virginia McKenzie. Virginia Temple. Daughter of Sarah Temple. Born in Sunnyside Nursing Home twenty-five years ago.'

She stood there while he gaped at her. Once he'd been handsome. Now he seemed weary of life, the lines of pain etched deeply on his face. But a light had come into his watery brown eyes and suddenly he was smiling.

'Virginia?' he quavered.

'Yes,' she said gently. 'You sent for me.'

'You are tall. Elegant. Blonde... Mary!' he groaned, covering his face with his hands.

Ginny flew to his side, forgetting the kind of man she'd been told he was, only knowing that he was deeply unhappy. Kneeling in front of him, she drew his hands away and held them in sympathy. 'What's upset you?' she asked in soft compassion.

Vincente studied her face intently. 'It doesn't matter now,' he said gruffly. 'You're here. And you are Mary's daughter. God forgive me for what I did! I've paid for my anger over and over!'

'Your... anger?' she said, thinking of his assault on his wife.

'Your mother and I quarrelled, Virginia,' he said in a low mutter. 'About Pascal. He's Susannah's son, you see.'

'Susannah's?' cried Ginny in astonishment. 'But... she's not old enough, surely—?'

'She was sixteen when he was born.' Vincente paused, staring into space, and his face showed the despair that he must have felt then. 'My cousin Louis seduced her,' he said grimly. 'Louis and I had always been rivals—he was engaged to your mother before me. When Mary fell for me and broke off the engagement, Louis turned to my sister for consolation.'

'And seduced her in revenge?' Ginny asked hesitantly.

Vincente looked into the distance as if searching his memory. 'I think they genuinely loved one another,' he admitted.

'I don't understand why you had to pretend Susannah's child was yours,' she probed.

Vincente sighed. 'To protect Susannah from the scandal. We decided to bring the child up as our own. We'd wanted a child for a long time. An heir to Beau Rivage.'

'I see.' Ginny knew only too well how important an heir was where dynastic families were concerned.

'Mary pretended she was pregnant. She stayed in the house to make the pretence easier. When Pascal was born, everyone believed he was our son.' He frowned. 'Unfortunately, Mary's enforced time indoors meant that it became increasingly hard for her to face going out and she developed a fear of open spaces.'

Ginny nodded, remembering that Leo had told her that Mary had suffered from agoraphobia—which had supposedly been caused by Vincente's ill-treatment. However, she believed Vincente's story about Mary gradually growing afraid of leaving the house till the problem had reached mammoth proportions. It made sense. She wondered if there was any connection with her mother's obsession with cleanliness. Perhaps she'd never know.

'How did Susannah feel about surrendering her baby?' she asked quietly.

'I never asked.' Vincente looked ashamed. 'We thought it was for the best,' he added, as if anxious not to appear callous. 'And we made sure she didn't get emotionally involved. A few years later, Mary said that Pascal should know who his mother was. I thought it was better not to rock the boat. We argued... Pascal was only six... He came in and found us yelling at each other. Pascal thought I was attacking her. I'm a monster in everyone's eyes,' he added gloomily.

Vincente's alleged brutality seemed unfounded. But something else had to be cleared up. The question burned on her lips. She had to have it answered. 'The rumour is,' said Ginny, taking a deep breath, 'that you flaunted your mistresses in front of your wife and that she ran away because you brought one into the house.'

The old man spread his hands in a gesture of helpless defeat. 'I know,' he said wearily. 'I admit I turned to other women. Mary wouldn't let me near her very often, you see—and I was a hot-blooded man in those days. I tried to be discreet, but this is a small island and news travels fast. People were only too delighted to tell Mary of my infidelity and I regret the pain I put her through.

'But the woman I brought into the house was not my mistress at all. She was supposed to be a companion for my wife because she wouldn't go out. I told her that but she refused to believe it. How can I ever prove that half the things said about me were lies?'

Ginny's face was soft with pity. 'You can't,' she said. 'Unless you find your wife. Wouldn't that help?'

'Yes!' cried Vincente, and she dearly wanted to believe his story because it would be a weight off her mind. He smiled weakly, his eyes devouring her from top to toe. 'You are so like her!'

He reached out his arms and drew Ginny to him, sobbing his heart out. Her own eyes grew moist and soon she was crying too. Vincente was friendless but he was a human being in distress and she probably carried his blood in her body. Overwhelmed by emotion, Ginny cradled him and rocked him till he'd regained control of himself.

'Do you really think I'm your daughter?' she asked tentatively. 'Really?'

Nicotine-stained fingers stroked her face with an extraordinary gentleness and awe. 'I know you are!' he declared. 'We must be sure, of course—do a DNA check... I *knew* Mandy wasn't the one. But the detective agency assured me—'

'Wait a minute,' she said, halting him in mid-flow. '*Mandy?* What do you mean?'

Vincente smiled and was overtaken by a fit of coughing. It was a while before he recovered and in that time Ginny shot a quick glance to the doorway. Leo was watching from the shadows, his face cold and full of hate. Ginny felt sick. Her worst fears had become a reality. Leo had a burning mission. Revenge—perhaps for something Vincente hadn't even done.

'Sorry,' croaked Vincente. 'Lungs. I'm dying, Virginia. That's why I wanted to find my child.'

'Oh, Vincente!' she cried, wide-eyed in dismay.

Her sympathy made him sigh. 'No one's spoken so caringly to me for a long time,' he said, choking with emotion. 'When I was led to believe that Mandy was my daughter, I hoped she would come to love me. Then I discovered she'd married Pascal. That almost broke my heart. I knew she'd side with him.' He saw Ginny's bewilderment and patted her hand. 'Mandy came from England in answer to my advert,' he explained. 'The detective agency I'd retained assured me she was Mary's daughter.'

'I see.' So Mandy had been the other woman who'd contacted the solicitor in London! 'Mandy and I *both* responded to your advert?'

'Yes. I've been searching for my daughter for a long time,' Vincente explained. 'I was so happy when Mandy arrived. She seemed so sweet and had all the right documents. Mary Brandon was given as her mother's name on her birth certificate.'

Ginny's eyebrows lifted. 'I don't understand—'

'Perhaps, Ginny,' came Leo's deep voice from behind them, 'Mary swapped her identity with Mandy's mother to make sure that Vincente never traced his real daughter.'

'Leo. My... husband,' said Ginny quickly, seeing Vincente's start of surprise. She was mulling over the suggestion, wondering if the idea had come from Leo's father. If it had, she thought it might possibly be true. Stuart Brandon knew a lot more than he'd let on, she decided. And one day she'd learn the whole story.

Vincente smiled, easing himself to his feet and extending his hand eagerly. 'My pleasure, Mr McKenzie. My very great pleasure. And perhaps you're right. In fact I have proof that Mandy isn't related to me so you must be, mustn't you?'

Ginny waited with bated breath. Leo would either stay true to his principles and denounce Vincente as a man unworthy of his regard or pretend that nothing was wrong. And she didn't know which of those she wanted him to do.

Leo hesitated for a fraction of a second before shaking Vincente's hand. 'How do you do?' he said formally. Because of his restraint, Ginny knew with a sinking feeling in the pit of her stomach that Leo was compromising his integrity in order to get his hands on Beau Rivage and to avenge Mary.

'You were saying,' said Leo idly, 'that you have proof that Mandy's claim is invalid?'

Vincente gripped Ginny's hand tightly. 'It's why I was so upset. I'd just had a telephone call from Pascal to say that the DNA tests prove Mandy doesn't have a drop of my blood in her. I was devastated by the news. I was feeling very sorry for myself.'

'How—how does Mandy feel about not being your daughter?' she asked tactfully.

'Pascal says she's delighted. So's he,' growled Vincente.

'They hate you,' she stated unhappily. 'He obviously thinks you treated your wife badly and he is ashamed of the women who keep coming here.'

Vincente snorted. 'Everyone thinks they're my mistresses,' he said wryly. 'Truth is, I haven't the energy any more. Haven't had it for years. I've been paying these young women well because I need companionship, I need someone to look after me and entertain me and they might as well be pretty. I'm lonely, you see.'

He sighed. 'Trouble is, they either expect marriage and a share in my fortune or can't stand the isolation. So they go running to Pascal and he pays them off and sends them home—if he hasn't bribed them to go already. Reputations aren't always deserved,' he said huskily.

'I know,' agreed Ginny with heartfelt fervour. 'I'll put Mandy and Pascal straight,' she promised.

'They'll still think badly of me,' Vincente said, almost inaudibly. 'Pascal believes I carelessly threw away a cigar and started the fire that killed his wife and child. He turned the whole community against me and he's loathed the sight of me ever since.' He took Ginny's face in his rough, planter's hands, and said earnestly, 'I didn't, Virginia. I wasn't anywhere near the house. It was someone else. You have to believe me—*you have to*!' he finished hoarsely.

Her pained eyes studied his. There was such anguish in his expression that she felt sure that he was telling the truth. 'I believe you.'

Vincente shuddered with relief. 'Thank God!' he said simply. 'If you hated and despised me too, I'd feel like killing myself. A few moments ago I thought I'd die without ever seeing my only child,' he added with a sentimental smile, stroking her silky hair in wonder. 'And then she walks in, just when I'm thinking that life's not worth living—'

'No!' she cried urgently. 'You mustn't think like that!'

'It's not true any more! We should celebrate,' said Vincente, his eyes shining with happiness. 'Champagne. It's in the cellar... Damn! I forgot my maid's left me—and the glasses are in the kitchen—'

'Are you all alone?' Ginny asked, shocked.

'Not any more,' Vincente answered softly.

'I'll get the champagne,' offered Leo, nothing in his voice betraying how he felt. Ginny shrugged off the chill that was wending its way down her spine. 'Ginny will find the glasses. Shall we celebrate outside?'

Vincente nodded, kissed Ginny warmly and directed them to the cellar and the kitchen. On emerging from the cellar Leo found her still searching for three glasses that weren't chipped.

'This place will be yours one day.'

She froze at Leo's flat tones, her hand on a cupboard door. Then she opened it and began to take down three Venetian flutes, obviously of great age and value. Washing them carefully and drying them on a glass cloth she'd found gave her time to compose her voice.

'I'm grateful to you for being so polite to him,' she said quietly. 'It must be an effort, considering.'

'How can you act as if you love him already?' he asked in soft reproach.

She whirled round, her eyes big and lustrous in the dark room. He was leaning against the doorjamb, his eyes dark and brooding. 'He's old and he's ill and he's genuinely sorry for what he's done. And he's not all bad. He's been misjudged. I think that's a shame and I want to reunite him with Pascal—even though they're not related.

'People make mistakes, Leo,' she said, her voice quivering with passion. 'I made a mistake. I know what he's going through, what remorse he's feeling. I think if you realise where you went wrong and badly want to make amends that you should have a second chance.'

They looked at one another for a breathless moment. And then he nodded curtly. 'Yes,' he said in a strangled rasp. 'You're right.'

'I want to live here, Leo,' she said flatly. 'I want to bring some joy into Vincente's life. He's dying and he's my father and he needs me.'

'I need you,' growled Leo.

'Oh? A woman who'll bring notoriety to the Brandons?' she asked bitterly. 'I think your motives are suspect. I believe you and your father are in some conspiracy to ensure that Beau Rivage becomes Brandon property.

'Would you give up Castlestowe for me? Do you love me so much that you'd throw away the land you've worked on all your life? Would you give up the social scene, the esteem with which everyone regards you and stay here with me?' The words were wobbling. She took a deep breath and steadied herself against the wooden draining-board. 'I think not, Leo,' she said, her heart breaking. Again. Because he'd leave her now. 'It means too much to you. I think not.'

And, unable to bear to think of losing him, she took the flutes in her hand and ran out to the veranda before she burst into tears.

They talked for the rest of the morning. Well, she and Vincente talked, telling each other about themselves. Leo sat silent, watching her as if mesmerised. And as if he was thinking out his future.

Eventually he offered to make lunch and surprised her by producing a sweet potato and pepper omelette with a plate of fruit to follow. In the afternoon Vincente went to sleep in his room, happily exhausted by the excitement.

Ginny and Leo followed Vincente's suggestion that they take two ponies and explore part of the estate. It suited her. She didn't want to talk to Leo or to hear his lies. Now that she'd given her ultimatum, he wouldn't marry her. Obviously he'd be leaving before dusk and the hours with him were precious and sweet.

Deliberately she lagged behind him when they galloped along the beautiful, deserted beach. What they'd seen had dismayed her. It would take a fortune to restore the plantation. Up in the valley, mill wheels, old slave quarters and sugar distilleries lay in ruins among frangipani trees and profusely flowering orchids. A sleeping paradise, occupied by one lonely and unhappy man.

Again she longed to seek out the truth of what had happened between Vincente and Mary and how they had become estranged. She knew now how easy that was when couples didn't communicate. Imagined affronts and misunderstandings grew in proportions till it was hard to take the first step towards reconciliation. And as a result her mother had run away and left Vincente with a reputation that had damned him.

She started. Leo had doubled back and had caught her pony's bridle.

'I want to talk to you,' he said quietly. 'Would you get down?' Nervously she obeyed. Leo studied her as if he'd never seen her before—perhaps as if he would never see her again. Her breath quickened in agitation. The moment to say goodbye had come, perhaps. 'Shall we sit in the shade?' he suggested, his voice sounding strangely husky.

'Mmm.' It was all she thought she could manage.

Leo sat a little way from her, staring out to sea. He pushed back his heavy silken hair with a quick gesture and she realised that he was tenser than he made out.

'What did you dislike most about our marriage?' he asked with studied casualness. But the hand he put on her arm was hot, as if it burned from a fire inside him.

'Your lifestyle,' she said nervously as the heat set her nerves dancing. 'Castlestowe, the closed world you moved in. It scared me. It never welcomed me.'

'Then for you I will give it up.'

Slowly Ginny turned her head. 'What?' she asked in astonishment. 'It means everything to you.'

He smiled and said lovingly, 'No. Not everything. I am prepared to give it up. I'm hoping you will abandon the thing *I* hated most—'

'My job?' Her puzzled face clouded. 'But...I want to do a little work each year. Not a lot, but perhaps some magazine-cover work—'

'It's not your job that was the problem,' he said softly. 'It was the fact that I hated being parted from you so much.'

'I would only take the occasional job. We could be together... But what's the point talking about it when you don't love me?' she said shakily. 'I won't be part of your revenge, Leo! I do want to be married. I love you so much. I can't pretend I don't. But you would hurt me every day by not loving me back. I would be nothing other than a convenience, a means to an end.

'You would be master of Beau Rivage. You would want us to have a child—children,' she amended jerkily when she saw the gleam in his eyes. 'A Brandon would own the plantation and your family honour would be satisfied. Where would I be once you'd achieved all that? Divorced? Abandoned for someone *suitable*, who would go back with you to bleak Castlestowe and act as a potential earl's wife should?

'I can't!' she wailed. 'I'd rather stay alone for the rest of my life than put my trust in you and have it flung back in my face! You have an ability to hide your feelings. To deceive. I don't know where I am with you and I can't marry you on such a shaky basis!'

'Ginny...' he began huskily, his tone almost cruelly loving.

'Don't coax me!' she stormed. 'I'm beyond coaxing! You wanted me to be Vincente's daughter! You said that knowing who I was would make a difference—'

'Sure. You'd be my financial and social equal—'

'And I'd be *suitable* then, would I?' she raged.

'Dammit, Ginny,' he said with a laugh. 'Let me finish! It's not that *I'd* care who you were, but that *you* would see yourself differently. No more believing you are inferior to me and my family! Because that's always been part of the trouble between us. You always *were* my equal!' he said affectionately. 'You didn't have to drive yourself into the ground earning a fortune and immense fame to prove that!'

'But... you only got interested in me again when you scented a chance to grab Beau Rivage!' she accused hysterically.

'Oh, no. I was always interested in you. Fascinated. Riveted. Bound to you, body, soul, mind, heart... Why the hell do you think I came over here, if it wasn't to win you back and protect you from a man my father said was a rogue?'

She covered her ears because it couldn't be true. 'I won't listen to you any more! Don't speak to me!'

Unable to bear looking at him any longer, she scrambled to her feet and turned away, walking a few steps into the tangled vegetation, her hand splayed out on the bark of a mahogany tree. And she breathed heavily, her whole body aching with misery.

'Stand very still,' Leo said suddenly in a strangely cracked voice.

Ginny frowned, began to turn her head, then saw by her outstretched hand the unmistakable head of an enormous snake. A boa constrictor. Only her eyes moved, growing larger and larger as the snake swayed its head with terrifying interest.

'Don't move an inch, my darling.'

As if she could! Panic had frozen her to the spot. Her horrified eyes made out yards of thick, muscled coils moving inexorably along a branch just above her head.

His voice came again. 'It's all right, darling. I'm here. I'll deal with it.'

She could hear Leo slowly, carefully treading on the soft jungle debris. He hated snakes, she thought. What could he do? They paralysed him with a morbid fear. He'd never touch it, would never—

The snake drew back its head. And suddenly she had been knocked to the ground, something sharp scoring down the length of her cheek. At first she thought it was the snake bite, but then she saw that Leo had his hands around the reptile's neck and was frantically trying to unwind the tightening coils from his bare arm.

She screamed, over and over again, slowly rising to her feet.

'You're safe now. Listen to me! I love you!' said Leo fiercely. 'For God's sake, Ginny, believe me! I'll eat this damn thing if it'll convince you! I love you and I always have! Believe me!'

Tears sprang to her eyes. To her astonishment, Leo smiled, then laughed exultantly and tightened his grip on the snake's throat. The coils flexed and loosened. With a grunt of disgust, he flung the boa into the bushes and she heard it softly slithering away.

Then Leo was tugging her to the beach and beneath the shade of a rustling palm. 'You believe me!' he murmured, kissing her.

'Of course I do!' she sobbed in relief. 'You rescued m-me from a s-s-snake when you loathe them . . .'

'I'd walk through fire for you. Oh, my darling,' he cried in alarm, touching her bleeding face. 'How did that happen? Your face! Your beautiful face! I can see some fragments of bark.' He brushed them away. 'A branch must have gone into it. It's deep, Ginny. We've got to get you to the hospital or you'll have a scar . . .'

'It doesn't matter,' she said with a shuddering sigh. 'It doesn't matter, Leo.' She smiled, kissing him. 'We'll wash it clean soon... But I don't care. My face isn't important any more.'

'It is! Your career—'

'No. *You* are important. You and Vincente.' She touched the livid bands on his arm, the imprints of the boa's scales clearly marked. 'You do love me. And I love you.'

'Yes,' he said passionately, kissing her again and again. 'I love you. With all my heart.'

'Then...will you live with me here?' she begged. 'Can you live with the man your family hates?'

'For you I can do anything, live anywhere, be anything,' he husked. 'I tried to protect you from Vincente because I couldn't bear to think of you being hurt in any way—not because of anything that might reflect on my family. That was an excuse to hide my real feelings.' He grinned lopsidedly. 'I'm crazy about you, Ginny!' he said fervently. 'I always have been, always will be.'

'Oh, Leo!' she sighed happily. 'And...you said that's why you came to St Lucia? Because you wanted me back?'

'Oh, yes. When I talked to Father and was told there was no doubt that you were Vincente's daughter, I wanted to be with you when you found out.' He smiled gently. 'I wanted to hold your hand, to help you cope with your emotions and whatever decision you came to. I thought you loved me—but I wasn't sure. I had to be sure. If I'd made a mistake it would have crucified me, Ginny. You mean so much to me.'

'I understand. I feel like that too. And...what of Castlestowe?' she asked anxiously.

'My estate manager can handle Castlestowe. He's doing that now, after all. I'll check progress every now and then. And I'll want to visit Grandfather, of course.'

'You'd...you'd really give up Castlestowe for me?' she asked, breathless with the idea.

'I'd give up everything for you. And don't imagine I'll pine for it. I know now where my happiness lies: with you. Mind you, it won't be easy living with Vincente. I'll have some adjusting to do.'

'I know,' she said soberly. 'But other than his early affairs—which I don't condone, of course—I don't think he's wicked. I'm sure he's been misunderstood. As you misunderstood my response to you when we made love and you accused me of—of learning from other men...'

'I'm sorry,' he said with regret. 'You seemed so uninhibited. I felt so jealous that I believed what Arabella had told me—that she'd seen lovers going to your room when you were both doing shows abroad—'

'Arabella!' she exclaimed indignantly. 'Leo, could she have circulated those rumours? She stood to benefit if I lost my popularity.'

He nodded, a frown marring his beautiful forehead. 'She certainly kept making sly digs about you. Forgive me,' he said simply.

'Nothing matters but the fact that you love me,' she said earnestly. 'We'll do what we can to clear my name, and Vincente's too—especially concerning that awful fire in which Pascal's child and his first wife died. And then—' she smiled, looking around at the tangled undergrowth '—we'll have our hands full helping Vincente set Rivage to rights. What do you think your father will think of that?'

Leo gave a short laugh. 'He'll have to take on the responsibility of the Castlestowe estate and limit his political ambition. He'll have to make choices, as I have. You can't have everything. There has to be a sacrifice.'

'He'll think you've betrayed him,' she said unhappily.

'No.' He kissed her mouth tenderly. 'Oddly enough, once he knew you were dead set on seeing Vincente he seemed to change his mind. I had a feeling that he was hoping we'd both live at Rivage. I'm not sure why. Perhaps because he wants it in the family, as you suggested. One day we might find out the truth. And one day we might trace your mother and—if she's still alive—hear the whole story.

'Oh, there's one thing, Ginny. I have a condition to make as far as living here is concerned.'

'Name it,' she said quietly. 'Whatever it is, we can talk it through.'

'Sure we can,' he answered, the love in his rich voice making her tremble with delight. His eyes twinkled wickedly. 'I do think we ought to get married, before anyone finds out we're not!'

Ginny giggled. And then she threw back her head and laughed with Leo, their laughter echoing across the silent bay.

'When we first married, I thought I knew what paradise could be,' Leo murmured huskily, kissing her lips with a heartbreaking sweetness. 'You and me living in the castle. I tried to make that come true but you kept dashing around the world. And then when I lost you I realised that I'd been wrong. I didn't need the castle at all. Only you. I worship you, Ginny,' he whispered passionately.

Ginny wound her arms around his neck. 'And I you.' She smiled. 'I wonder if Chas will come here with his family when his wife and baby can travel?' she mused. 'Oh, Leo, I want your baby!' she said with a sudden urgency.

Their lips met, emotion deepening their kiss. And she thought of their children running free on Beau Rivage and sighed with pleasure at the thought that she and Leo would be bringing joy and love and compassion into Vincente's life. She had a father. A husband she loved with all her heart. Friends in Pascal and Mandy. Soon a child would come and her life would be complete.

That was all that mattered. Love of friends, family and someone very, very special. She and Leo. Together, for always.

* * * * *

Look out for Amber's story
in AMBER'S WEDDING,
available next month.

1998

| SUNDAY | MONDAY | TUESDAY | WEDNESDAY | THURSDAY | FRIDAY | SATURDAY |

Keep track of important dates

Three beautiful and colorful calendars that celebrate some of the most popular trends in America today.

Look for:

Just Babies—a 16 month calendar that features a full year of absolutely adorable babies!

Hometown Quilts—a 16 month calendar featuring quilted art squares, plus a short history on twelve different quilt patterns.

Inspirations—a 16 month calendar with inspiring pictures and quotations.

STEEPLE HILL™

◆ HARLEQUIN®

Value priced at $9.99 U.S./$11.99 CAN., these calendars make a perfect gift!

Available in retail outlets in August 1997.   CAL98

Take 4 bestselling love stories FREE

Plus get a FREE surprise gift!

Special Limited-time Offer

Mail to Harlequin Reader Service®

    3010 Walden Avenue
    P.O. Box 1867
    Buffalo, N.Y. 14240-1867

YES! Please send me 4 free Harlequin Presents® novels and my free surprise gift. Then send me 6 brand-new novels every month, which I will receive months before they appear in bookstores. Bill me at the low price of $2.90 each plus 25¢ delivery and applicable sales tax, if any*. That's the complete price and a savings of over 10% off the cover prices—quite a bargain! I understand that accepting the books and gift places me under no obligation ever to buy any books. I can always return a shipment and cancel at any time. Even if I never buy another book from Harlequin, the 4 free books and the surprise gift are mine to keep forever.

106 BPA A3UL

Name	(PLEASE PRINT)

Address	Apt. No.

City	State	Zip

This offer is limited to one order per household and not valid to present Harlequin Presents® subscribers. *Terms and prices are subject to change without notice. Sales tax applicable in N.Y.

UPRES-696   ©1990 Harlequin Enterprises Limited

Every month there's another title from one
of your favorite authors!

October 1997
Romeo in the Rain by Kasey Michaels
When Courtney Blackmun's daughter brought home Mr. Tall,
Dark and Handsome, Courtney wanted to send the young
matchmaker to her room! Of course, that meant the single
New Jersey mom would be left alone with the irresistibly
attractive Adam Richardson....

November 1997
Intrusive Man by Lass Small
Indiana's Hannah Calhoun had enough on her hands taking
care of her young son, and the last thing she needed was a
man complicating things—especially Max Simmons, the
gorgeous cop who had eased himself right into her little boy's
heart…and was making his way into hers.

December 1997
Crazy Like a Fox by Anne Stuart
Moving in with her deceased husband's—*eccentric*—family
in Louisiana meant a whole new life for Margaret Jaffrey and
her nine-year-old daughter. But the beautiful young widow
soon finds herself seduced by the slower pace and the much-
too-attractive cousin-in-law, Peter Andrew Jaffrey....

**BORN IN THE USA: Love, marriage—
and the pursuit of family!**

Available at your favorite retail outlet!

Free Gift Offer

As Seen on TV!

With a Free Gift proof-of-purchase
from any Harlequin® book, you can receive
a beautiful cubic zirconia pendant.

This stunning marquise-shaped stone is a genuine cubic
zirconia—accented by an 18" gold tone necklace.
(Approximate retail value $19.95)

Send for yours today...
compliments of 🌹HARLEQUIN®

To receive your free gift, a cubic zirconia pendant, send us one original proof-of-purchase, photocopies not accepted, from the back of any Harlequin Romance®, Harlequin Presents®, Harlequin Temptation®, Harlequin Superromance®, Harlequin Intrigue®, Harlequin American Romance®, or Harlequin Historicals® title available at your favorite retail outlet, together with the Free Gift Certificate, plus a check or money order for $1.65 U.S./$2.15 CAN. (do not send cash) to cover postage and handling, payable to Harlequin Free Gift Offer. We will send you the specified gift. Allow 6 to 8 weeks for delivery. Offer good until December 31, 1997, or while quantities last. Offer valid in the U.S. and Canada only.

Free Gift Certificate

Name: _____

Address: _____

City: _____ State/Province: _____ Zip/Postal Code: _____

Mail this certificate, one proof-of-purchase and a check or money order for postage and handling to: HARLEQUIN FREE GIFT OFFER 1997. In the U.S.: 3010 Walden Avenue, P.O. Box 9071, Buffalo NY 14269-9057. In Canada: P.O. Box 604, Fort Erie, Ontario L2Z 5X3.

FREE GIFT OFFER   084-KEZ

ONE PROOF-OF-PURCHASE

To collect your fabulous FREE GIFT, a cubic zirconia pendant, you must include this original proof-of-purchase for each gift with the properly completed Free Gift Certificate.

084-KEZR

Don't miss these Harlequin favorites
by some of our bestselling authors! Act now and
receive a discount by ordering two or more titles!

HT#25720	A NIGHT TO REMEMBER	$3.50 U.S. ☐
	by Gina Wilkins	$3.99 CAN. ☐
HT#25722	CHANGE OF HEART	$3.50 U.S. ☐
	by Janice Kaiser	$3.99 CAN. ☐
HP#11797	A WOMAN OF PASSION	$3.50 U.S. ☐
	by Anne Mather	$3.99 CAN. ☐
HP#11863	ONE-MAN WOMAN	$3.50 U.S. ☐
	by Carole Mortimer	$3.99 CAN. ☐
HR#03356	BACHELOR'S FAMILY	$2.99 U.S. ☐
	by Jessica Steele	$3.50 CAN. ☐
HR#03441	RUNAWAY HONEYMOON	$3.25 U.S. ☐
	by Ruth Jean Dale	$3.75 CAN. ☐
HS#70715	BAREFOOT IN THE GRASS	$3.99 U.S. ☐
	by Judith Arnold	$4.50 CAN. ☐
HS#70729	ANOTHER MAN'S CHILD	$3.99 U.S. ☐
	by Tara Taylor Quinn	$4.50 CAN. ☐
HI#22361	LUCKY DEVIL	$3.75 U.S. ☐
	by Patricia Rosemoor	$4.25 CAN. ☐
HI#22379	PASSION IN THE FIRST DEGREE	$3.75 U.S. ☐
	by Carla Cassidy	$4.25 CAN. ☐
HAR#16638	LIKE FATHER, LIKE SON	$3.75 U.S. ☐
	by Mollie Molay	$4.25 CAN. ☐
HAR#16663	ADAM'S KISS	$3.75 U.S. ☐
	by Mindy Neff	$4.25 CAN. ☐
HH#28937	GABRIEL'S LADY	$4.99 U.S. ☐
	by Ana Seymour	$5.99 CAN. ☐
HH#28941	GIFT OF THE HEART	$4.99 U.S. ☐
	by Miranda Jarrett	$5.99 CAN. ☐

(limited quantities available on certain titles)

TOTAL AMOUNT	$ _____
DEDUCT: **10% DISCOUNT FOR 2+ BOOKS**	$ _____
POSTAGE & HANDLING	$ _____
($1.00 for one book, 50¢ for each additional)	
APPLICABLE TAXES*	$ _____
TOTAL PAYABLE	$ _____

(check or money order—please do not send cash)

To order, complete this form and send it, along with a check or money order for the total above, payable to Harlequin Books, to: **In the U.S.:** 3010 Walden Avenue, P.O. Box 9047, Buffalo, NY 14269-9047; **In Canada:** P.O. Box 613, Fort Erie, Ontario, L2A 5X3.

Name: _____

Address: _____ City: _____

State/Prov.: _____ Zip/Postal Code: _____

*New York residents remit applicable sales taxes.
Canadian residents remit applicable GST and provincial taxes.

Look us up on-line at: http://www.romance.net   HBKOD97